By the Same Author

BRING TO A BOIL AND SEPARATE
MOON & ME
WHAT ABOUT GRANDMA?
I BE SOMEBODY
(MARGARET K. MCELDERRY BOOKS)

THE LILITH SUMMER
WE ARE MESQUAKIE, WE ARE ONE

Abby,
My Love

Abby,
My Love

Hadley Irwin

A Margaret K. McElderry Book
ATHENEUM **1985** **NEW YORK**

Lines from "The Hill" and "Lucinda Matlock" from SPOON RIVER ANTHOLOGY by Edgar Lee Masters (Copyright © 1914, 1915 by William Marion Reedy. Copyright © 1915, 1916, 1942 and 1944 by Edgar Lee Masters) and lines from "Unknown Soldiers" from THE NEW SPOON RIVER ANTHOLOGY by Edgar Lee Masters (Copyright © 1924 by Edgar Lee Masters) reprinted with the kind permission of Mrs. Ellen C. Masters.

Library of Congress Cataloging in Publication Data
Irwin, Hadley.
Abby, my love.
"A Margaret K. McElderry book."
Summary: In love since junior high, Chip and Abby finally share Abby's secret: her father is sexually abusing her.
[1. Child abuse—Fiction. 2. Incest—Fiction]
I. Title.
PZ7.I712Ab 1985   [Fic]   84-24571
ISBN 0-689-50323-7

*To Margaret K.
In whom we trust*

Our special thanks to Anna Stone,
Social Service Supervisor, Division of Family Services,
Liberty, Missouri,

and to Jeanne Beardsley,
Clinical Social Worker, Central Iowa Mental Health Center,
Ames, Iowa,
for their professional advice.

Abby,
My Love

Valedictory

*A*BIGAIL MORRIS."
I watched her cross the stage, her white robe blowing in the June breeze, her auburn hair tucked beneath her mortar board. She looked as cool as a frosty mint julep, a drink I had decided was sophisticated enough for me as a college man finishing my freshman year.

Abby stood, poised and smiling, as the principal began listing the awards and honors she had achieved. "Already voted by the consensus of opinion of her classmates most likely to succeed, Abigail has also earned the following honors: Iowa Women's Club Citizenship Award . . ."

My head clicked off. If Abby were a mint julep, I was a hot toddy. I was frying. It must have been 105 degrees in the Collinsville High School gym. My pants stuck to

1

the metal folding chair. Only for Abby had I given up my levis for polyester.

Her head was tilted and the smile still on her lips, but I knew she wasn't really there on stage. Even from where I sat, sweltering, I could see the empty look in her eyes. Once it had puzzled me. It had taken me five years to learn that it meant Abby was gone—absent—not available. She was pulled back so far inside that she was in a different world to which no one ever gained admittance —except me. Once.

"And as the valedictorian of this graduating class," the principal continued, "a high honor, irregardless of the other awards she has won . . ."

Abby's eyes switched back on, and very slowly, so slowly that no one else could have noticed, she winked down at me. Old Redundant had done it again. Abby and I must have spent half our high school years together keeping track of the illiteracies in Principal Boylan's speeches. "Consensus of opinion" and "irregardless" were his favorites. The day he broke the record, five mistakes in three minutes, we laughed so hard we both had to spend a half-hour after school in detention.

"Abigail is our finest example of the highest qualities that Collinsville High stands for." Old Redundant was finally running down.

No one but the principal and Abby's father called her "Abigail."

"I hate my name!" she told me once.

"Don't see why. It's a pretty name. Means 'source of joy.' "

"How do you know?"

I'll never forget the look she gave me as if I had discovered something I shouldn't have.

"I looked it up in the back of my dictionary. Wasn't looking for your name, anyway. Was looking for my own: Chip. Wasn't even on the list."

I called her "Abigail" once after that, just to tease. She turned and looked at me as if I'd said a dirty word, and she didn't talk to me for three days. I never called her Abigail again.

I glanced down at the commencement program. Abby's valedictory speech was next. We had already sat through the main speaker, a professor of education from the state university whose topic covered half the page: "Cybernetics, a Heuristically Holistic View of the Future."

I tugged at my shirt collar until it occurred to me I wasn't wearing a tie. Even for Abby that was too much. Mom elbowed me in the ribs, pointed to the list of seniors and rolled her eyes. "One hundred forty-seven?"

I patted her knee and whispered, "Sit still and be a good girl and you can have ice cream afterwards."

She elbowed me again, harder, and tried not to grin.

"Faculty, parents, and students," Abby began, and everyone listened. It was hard not to because there was something about her voice that caught your attention whether you were willing to listen or not. In all my nineteen years I'd never heard another voice quite like it, and after a year of college, I'd heard lots of girls' voices. Sometimes they were high and squeaky; some of them sounded like dripping butter or warm syrup. Not Abby's. Hers was husky and soft unless she got mad or excited, and then it cracked just like mine used to when I was growing up. From my mouth it sounded dumb, but from Abby's it sounded . . . well, it sounded enchanting. That was a word I'd never use aloud, maybe because, in my mind, it belonged only to Abby. Funny, I'd never told

3

her that. She knew almost everything else about me though.

"We are not alone. We are not powerless." The gym darkened, and she stood in the center of a circle of light. "We control our own lives."

Two rows ahead of me, Abby's mother sat up straighter. Beside her, Pete, perched on the edge of her chair as if she were going to rush on stage and proclaim to the world, "She's my sister!" was wearing the tennis sweatband I had brought her back from college. I wondered how she'd got away with that.

Abby's father was not there.

"Nothing that happens to us affects only us. Nothing we do affects only ourselves. We belong to the world, and the world belongs to us."

For once I didn't listen. I didn't have to. Abby had mailed me a copy of her speech as soon as she knew she was valedictorian. I knew her words by heart.

Chapter One

I FELL IN LOVE when I was thirteen. I fell in love sitting on a swing in Edgewater Park, dragging my sneakers in the dust and trying for the hundredth time to figure out how to convince Mom that if I didn't go out for junior high football my entire life would be ruined.

One minute I was sitting in the swing picking a scab off my knee; the next minute I was sitting in the dust and the wooden seat of the swing was bouncing off my head. When I turned around to see what had sent me flying, there she was: curly red hair, long silky eyelashes, violet eyes, just as violet as Elizabeth Taylor's in that old movie *National Velvet*, and a body that was exactly the way it should be.

"What are you doing down there? You should be more

careful." Her voice sounded kind of like a gravelly music box.

"What do you mean, what am I doing? What are you doing? Don't you ever watch where you're going?" I stood up and dusted myself off.

"I'm practicing."

"Practicing what?"

"Running backwards."

"Who are you?" Standing beside me she was even smaller than I'd thought at first.

"I'm Pete."

It happened just that fast. I was in love with a girl named Pete. What made it even worse, she looked about six years old. It was only worse for a minute or two. Then I met Abby.

"She belong to you?" I growled, running my hand through my hair to see if my head was bleeding.

"She's my little sister."

I looked at Abby and forgot all about concussions— and Pete. Abby had the deepest, darkest eyes I had ever seen. I guess all I saw were her eyes. I tried to think of somthing to say, but my head was whirling. I looked down at the ground, wondering how kids always scuff off a perfect oval in the dirt under a playground swing.

"What's she practicing running backwards for?"

Abby wasn't having any trouble looking at me. I could feel it. "Pete wants to be a baseball player. Chicago Cubs."

"But she's a girl!" I said, without thinking.

"So?" She shrugged.

"So?" I repeated. "Who are you, anyway?"

"Abby Morris. I'm twelve."

"I'm thirteen! You live here?"

"We moved here a year ago. My father is a dentist, and we moved into our new house last week. I went to Greeley Grade School last year, but I'm going to be in Wilson Junior High this fall. I'll be in seventh grade."

"I'm in eighth grade!" Words came out of my mouth in jerks and rushes, sort of like the way a car runs on bad spark plugs. "You like baseball too? Like your kid sister?"

"Yes. I think it is an interesting sport to watch or to read about. After all it's our national game. I read once that Washington's soldiers played it at Valley Forge. I didn't really believe that, though, because I thought it always snowed at Valley Forge."

Listening to Abby talk was like listening to the engine of a finely tuned sports car, a Porsche or a Lamborghini. Most of the time she spoke in whole sentences, maybe even paragraphs, not at all like the other kids my age. It was kind of eerie, really. There she was, only twelve years old, but she sounded so much older, like she was an adult and I was the kid. She wasn't condescending or anything. She was just different.

"Do you like football?"

I wasn't comfortable, but I had to keep thinking up questions so she'd stick around.

"Physical contact is Neanderthal! Twenty-two men fighting over a little ball is really quite juvenile."

"What *do* you like?" I was running out of questions.

"I think cricket is an interesting game. It's sort of like baseball only they have wickets instead of bases." She looked at her watch and frowned. "I must be going now. It's been nice to meet you."

That's what I mean. Kids never say goodby to each other that way. I grabbed at something else to say, something to keep her around a little longer. "Man! That's some watch."

It was. I'd seen one just like it in *The New Yorker* magazine. Mom took *The New Yorker* and made me read it so I wouldn't get culture shock if I ever got out of Collinsville. Anyway, it wasn't a Timex or some other kid watch. It was a Rollex and must have cost about nine million dollars.

Abby looked down at it again as if it were some kind of bug crawling on her arm. "My father gave it to me, so I have to wear it. I think it looks like a handcuff."

Then she was gone, and I was left standing there, one hand holding the cold chain of the swing.

I was late getting home that night. There was only one thing that Mom insisted on. That's not quite right. Mom seldom insisted. She suggested, but one strict rule was that I must start the dinner. The menu was tacked up on the refrigerator door with little magnetic clips and neat little check marks after what I was supposed to do. Tonight the menu was grilled steaks and salad. I was to make the salad. I could have tossed a dozen salads, could have tossed them all over the kitchen. I'd just dropped in the last artichoke heart when Mom walked in.

"He's gone bonkers! My only beloved son is smiling at a tossed salad!" She staggered dramatically to the refrigerator and clutched the door. "Quickly, a drink. Iced tea. A cold cloth for my brow."

My mother was weird, but I was used to it. I kept waiting for her to grow up, but she never did. Of course, she had her own business, and she'd raised me by herself, and she could be serious at times; but mostly when we were together, we were the same age.

8

I got her tea and she looked at me with a raised eyebrow. "Okay, out with it. You've thought of the one perfect, indisputable reason for playing football."

I hoisted myself up on the kitchen counter. "Nope. Physical contact is Neanderthal. Maybe baseball. An outfielder, maybe."

Now both of Mom's eyebrows were raised. "But you hate baseball. You won't even watch the World Series. You never collected baseball cards. I'll bet you don't even know the names of the major league teams."

I didn't, except for the Chicago Cubs.

"It has to be a girl. Don't tell me at long last my son has discovered a girl!"

"Not a girl. Girls," I said.

"Girls then. Where'd you meet them? What're they like? Where do they live?" Mom set down her tea and leaned back in her chair.

"Well," I began. "One's little . . . and cute . . . and . . ."

"Don't tell me. I know. She likes baseball." Mom folded her arms as if she were still in her office and had just signed up a client for a round-the-world cruise. Mom runs a travel agency downtown. Not only runs it, owns it.

"How'd you know she likes baseball?" I grinned.

"Guessed. So she's little and cute and likes baseball?"

"Yeah." I slid off the counter. "Only thing is, Mom. She isn't very old . . . yet."

Mom reached for her glass again, then stopped. "What do you mean yet? How old is she?"

"I don't know. Six maybe."

"I trust you haven't asked her for a date."

I could feel the red creep up my neck, even though

I knew she was just kidding. Ever since I could remember, whenever I was embarrassed, I blushed, which is bad enough any time, but worse if you are well on your way to being six feet tall. Mom said my dad blushed like that too, and that's why she had married him. Personally, I'd almost rather have acne. At least people grew out of that.

"Don't want to date her. Maybe we could sort of rent her on weekends or after school. A little sister would be good for me. Teach me responsibility. I'd have to be a role model. Wouldn't it be nice to have a little kid around?"

I didn't say it, but I was thinking Pete had a definite plus, and that plus was Abby.

"Chipster." Mom looked kind of cute when she gritted her teeth. "Do you remember your cousin Candi?"

"Yes."

No one could forget Candi. We saw her at least once a year when we went skiing in Colorado. Candi was a mouthy, stupid, hateful little brat, whom we both despised. She was Mom's godchild. Candi was six years old too.

"And this new love has a sister?"

I felt the red creep up again.

"Well . . . yes. Her sister is named Abby. She's twelve, but she acts like thirty."

"Let's eat." Mom stood up. "We'll talk about the rent-a-kid program later."

Mom thought I'd been kidding about Pete, but in a way I wasn't. I had always hated being an only child. I had to go out and find someone to play with, especially now when my best friend, Rob, was on vacation. I dreamed of having brothers and sisters, but Mom had

10

explained when I was five all that stuff of how you get babies. "It takes a Mommy and a Daddy, and your daddy was lost in Vietnam."

So from the time I was six I kept hunting for a prospective daddy. I tried everyone from the garbage man to the mail carrier to the school crossing guard. All of them were either too old, too young, or already married, and besides, Mom was never interested. That didn't stop me from wanting, because most of all I wanted a brother or a sister, and I couldn't think of any other way to get one.

That night, after an hour's search, I found my outfielder's mitt in the back of my closet under my outgrown ice skates. I figured baseball would be easier than cricket.

It didn't take me long to find out when they came to the park. Every day it was the same, except on weekends: from four until Abby's father rang a big old bell that he'd found at some antique store. It sounded like a church bell, and he had it mounted on a post by their patio. Even today, the sound of a bell starts something aching down under my ribs because Abby and Pete always stopped whatever we were playing and ran for home as if they were being pulled. They lived in the big house down at the dead end of our block, where it curled around in a cul de sac.

Pete and I became friends. We played catch and "pump up" on the swings, hunted frogs down in the little pond, and climbed the maple tree, pretending we were explorers in a jungle. I didn't make much headway with Abby. She sat. Sometimes she read a book, and sometimes Kriss Ames, who lived farther down our block and was in Abby's grade, came with her. Kriss wasn't a

11

bad kid, not as silly as some twelve year olds, but she wasn't very interesting either—probably because I'd known her all my life.

The last few weeks before school started, summer sort of sagged toward September, and Rob hadn't come back from vacation yet.

That afternoon I was down in the park playing catch with Pete. Abby was around too, somewhere. That was the funny thing. It was like Abby was Pete's mother. You'd see Pete, and there'd be Abby, just as if she couldn't let her out of her sight. I had just managed to nab a wild throw from Pete when I heard Rob's Tarzan yell. I was so glad to see him I dropped the ball and threw my glove in the air.

Rob came wheeling in on his bike and braked it real hard, so the front wheel spun up into the air. "Come on. Get your bike. I'll race you to the football field."

"Can I come too?" Pete ran up and tugged at my shirt. "I can go get my bike."

"Not this time. Go play with Abby." I felt kind of mean, but I hadn't seen Rob for a month. I left Pete standing there, scowling at me, her hands on her hips, but Abby was walking over to her so I figured she'd take care of the kid's feelings.

I ran home and got my bike, and Rob and I took off. We were coasting down the hill past Wilson Junior High when Rob yelled, "Race you round the track." Rob beat me. I could have won, but I didn't feel like it. Sometimes it's no fun to beat someone you like a lot. Rob and I had been pals through Cub Scouts, summer camps, Little League, and a whole long year of Mrs. Buckel's sixth grade.

We climbed up into the bleachers. The sun was a big

12

red ball hanging like a balloon over the trees that fringed the field.

"Who're the new kids?" Rob squinted off into the sun.

I stared down at my knees. It's funny how it's kind of hard to look right at someone you like a lot, especially when you haven't seen him for a while.

"Pete and Abby Morris. Their dad's a dentist. They just moved into the neighborhood."

"Hey." Rob leaned back against the bleacher seat and stretched out his legs. "I know him."

"How come?"

"I had to get a check-up before we left. Our dentist was out of town, so Mom had me go to Dr. Morris. He's sort of a funny guy."

I had never thought about Pete's and Abby's folks. Pete and Abby were so different, I couldn't imagine what their parents were like. Of course, I'd seen their mother jogging past our house every morning early, in a different jogging suit every time.

"What do you mean, funny?"

"You know how dentists are. Asking questions all the time and you're lying there with your mouth full of their hands."

"I sure wouldn't want to be a dentist," I said leaning back like Rob. "Can you imagine looking down people's throats all day? All those teeth? All those wet tongues?"

Rob looked over at me, rolled his eyes and smirked. "You didn't seem to mind Karen's that time!"

Rob never forgot anything. He had something like a photographic memory, which was one reason he got such good grades in school, but right then I was wishing he wouldn't use it about other things that I would like to have forgotten. He was remembering a party at Karen's where some of the kids came up with some stupid game called "Dare You." Two people were supposed to do whatever was on a piece of paper that you drew out of a hat. Karen and I had to stick our tongues in each other's mouths.

"I didn't like it! Karen didn't either. Messy and boring."

"Maybe it depends who the other person is. On TV they make it look like fun."

Rob was so serious I was pretty sure he'd been thinking about such things a lot.

"Girls are funny," I said. "You never know what they're thinking, and I never know what to talk about."

"Me neither."

It was funny. I could talk to Mom, but then she was a woman, and I could have fun with Pete, but something happened to me when I had to talk to girls my own age. One day they were just somebody in your grade, then suddenly they turned into girls and it was sort of scary.

"Well, I got to go." Rob stood up. "I'm supposed to help unpack the camper."

We started down from the bleachers. "Did I miss anything when I was gone?"

"Nothing much. Oh. Did you hear what happened to Principal Boylan's car at the last softball game?"

"No."

"Somebody jacked it up. You won't believe it. These high school guys. Twelve of them. You know the bunch. Well, they made a kind of human chain and dismantled Boylan's WHOLE transmission from his VW and carried it off. Only took them ten minutes. They learned how in shop. In school."

14

"How'd they get away with that?"

"Parking lot was dark and they worked fast. My mom heard about it too. She said somebody told her they were sending the parts back to him, one at a time, C.O.D."

"Dumb!"

"I guess," I agreed. "Funny, though, don't you think?"

"Not really. Not for Mr. Boylan." I couldn't figure it out. Rob usually laughed at things like that.

He straddled his bike and stood there fiddling with the brake lever and teetering from one foot to the other. It was the quietest time of the day, somewhere around five, when the world almost stops for a breath and all the sound seeps out, no screen doors slamming, no kids hollering, even the birds sort of run out of songs. Maybe that was why Rob's voice sounded so loud.

"We're going to move, you know."

"You're what?"

"We're moving. To California."

"When?"

"Before school starts."

"But that's next week!" I felt as if a big high school kid had punched me out.

"I know."

What had been so quiet before was now a funny kind of ringing in my ears, as if his voice were bouncing off a wall. I tried to grin, but my face felt tight.

"You got to be kidding." It came out in a kind of growl.

Rob didn't answer. He put his weight on the pedals and rode away. I didn't follow. I just stood there staring at my sneakers and trying to think of something to think.

Chapter Two

I GAVE UP GIRLS when I was fourteen, or maybe they gave me up. Whichever way it was, it all amounted to the same thing.

That year we formed our club. It wasn't a club like school counselors are always trying to get started—photography club or science club or Spanish club—with officers and minutes and all that stuff. It wasn't a gang, either. It was just a bunch of us guys who started hanging around together. We had only one rule: No Girls! That was Chub Prentiss's idea.

It all started that fall when we had to elect eighth grade class officers. All the girls in our class wanted Karen for president. We guys didn't, so we got together down in the locker room and planned it.

"We'll nominate three or four more girls besides

16

Karen," Chub said, crouched down on his knees as if he were plotting out the next football play. "Then Chip, you nominate old Marv here. Just Marv. No one else. Then I'll move that nominations cease. That way we'll split the girl's vote."

I'm not sure why I went along with it, but at the time it seemed fun. We railroaded our whole slate through, not only president, but vice-president, secretary, and treasurer. I was vice-president. I guess that was the first time I'd tasted power and it tasted good.

"We can run things this year," Chub insisted, "if we stick together."

And that's how the MP Club got started, MP for Man Power. We didn't hold meetings or anything like that, but we had a secret sign: a clenched fist and a quick brush at a fellow MP's chin. We kept our membership at five: Chub, Marv, Shikes, Mike and me. We adopted tee shirts, blue jeans, and dirty sneakers as our uniforms and let our hair grow. We always sat together at lunch, and after school we'd get on our bikes and circle the school grounds once before taking off for home, jumping curbs and doing wheelies. Studying was for stupes. Books for wimps. Baths for babies. Girls for committees.

That was when Mom almost stopped speaking to me. Abby DID stop speaking to me—completely.

"Chip Martin! Would you mind combing your hair? Just once. And let me trim it there in front," Mom suggested as I sprawled across the sofa. "You're going to ruin your eyes trying to squint through that mop."

"Get off my back, will you? What's wrong with my hair? I'm just letting it grow natural."

"Natural," she repeated, her voice increasing in decibels. "You look like a sheep dog. Get your feet off my davenport and throw out those awful sneakers. They smell."

"Anything else wrong with me?" I asked, rolling off onto the rug.

"Yes. You're a complete slob. What's gotten into you? I can't force you into a shower. You're too big. What's with this back-to-nature look?"

"What do you want me to do? Wear a shirt and tie? Get a crew cut?"

Mom stood over me. "Did you take a good look at your grades this semester?"

I knew I was in for it. Actually, they were sort of pretty. Uniform, at least. A series of semi-circles with a minus now and then for variety.

"You've never had a C before in your life."

"What's wrong with C's? More C people in the world than anything else. That's why it's average."

"Thanks a lot for the explanation. I didn't realize you were capable of such logic."

I couldn't stand Mom when she tried to be sarcastic.

"Look, Chip. Seriously." She sank back into the recliner. "Is there something wrong or are you going through the 'barely-human' stage?"

"How should I know. Never been this old before. Besides, that's your business. You're the mother."

"I'm seriously thinking of resigning. And I'm beginning to understand what an 'unwanted child' is."

We had always kidded back and forth, Mom and I, but this was different. For some reason I wanted to say things that would hurt her, but I couldn't tell her that because I didn't know why I felt that way. I'd thought about it a lot. It was sort of an ugly, mean feeling, down

18

deep, so that I felt good after I'd really lashed out at somebody. Not felt good, really. Felt satisfied. Then there was another thing. I didn't like the way I looked. My arms were too long, my legs too short, my head too little, my shoulders too broad. I was sure I looked like a half-grown ape.

"Honey," Mom tried again. "Is it Rob? You were such good friends. I know you miss him."

I got up and turned on TV. "I have other friends."

"Yes, I know. The problem is they all smell like you."

I can't remember when it was, maybe it was sometime in the spring. It must have been because I was walking home from school. I'd bent the frame on my bike jumping curbs and Mom had said I'd have to figure out how to get another bike on my own. I spotted Pete coming out of the grade school, and for once she didn't have a bunch of other kids tagging along.

I said there was a big difference between Pete and Abby and that was one. Abby had friends, of course, but only one or two at a time. Pete usually had all the neighborhood kids trailing after her. I didn't see much of Abby that year; after all she was a girl, but I hadn't forgotten her. Once in a while I'd catch a glimpse of her in school and it could have been a scene from a movie about outer space. There was kind of a light around her, a shimmer. For me, she glowed. I couldn't understand why, but it was real.

Anyway, I caught up with Pete. She didn't hear me coming, and I moved up behind her and put both hands over her eyes.

She didn't even jump. She just said, "Hi, Chip.'

19

I let her go. "How'd you know?"

She stopped walking and stood there looking up at me with her fists on her hips. "I didn't have to SEE you. I could SMELL you."

If she'd been Mom, I would have ignored her and stomped on down the street. If she'd been a boy and not too big, I'd have socked her.

"Listen, twerp. That's no way to talk. You're supposed to respect your elders. Besides, you're sweating so much I can't see how you could smell anything."

She was. She was dripping from some last-minute pick-up ball game on the playground. Funny, though, she just looked damp and smelled like mown grass. I wondered if all girls were like that. If they were, they were lucky.

"You coming to the game tomorrow? I'm planning on hitting a homer. Dalton's got a lousy pitcher."

One thing about Pete, she at least hadn't changed. She still loved baseball, and she was still talking to me.

"Sure, I'll come. Me and my buddies." I was at the place where I hardly ever did anything alone. It was easier being with the other guys, that way I sort of blended in.

"I don't like your buddies. They stink too. Sure glad I'm not your mother."

"Don't sweat it, kid. You're too young."

"And you're not nice anymore." She hopped along beside me, avoiding the cracks in the walk. "And," she said, turning to face me, "Abby thinks you're a big creep! So there! And we figured out what MP means. Macho Poops!"

"I should care what Abby thinks." But I did care.

"See," I went on. "What I'm doing is called growing up.

20

And if you think it's easy, just wait a few years. Sometimes I don't like me much either." Somehow I could
say the words to Pete that I couldn't say to Mom.

"If you don't like you, why don't you change back?"

"It's not like learning to run backwards. Growing up
means you have to go ahead."

We were in front of my house by then.

"Well, can't you hurry up and get there?" she hol-
lered back at me as she dashed down the block toward
home.

That night I did take a shower without Mom's even
suggesting it.

I sure didn't change over night like a frog into a
prince. I tried hard to pretend that what Pete had said
didn't make any difference because, after all, she was
just a kid, but what Abby thought did matter. Sometimes, though, all you need is a little nudge at the right
time. Three things happened and there I was sort of like
a male Alice in Wonderland, only I was going up the
rabbit hole instead of down, and it started with a beer
party, not a tea party.

That Friday, we'd had a school assembly on the dan-
gers of drugs and alcohol. It was interesting, really. This
guy had been into the booze when he was young and, as
he told us, "wasted his life in riotous living," and now he
went around to schools to warn kids against smoking the
first cigarette and taking the first sip of liquor. He poured
out a glass of beer right up there on the stage and
dropped a worm in it. Of course, the worm curled up
and died. I got to thinking later it would have probably
done the same thing in a glass of ice water.

It was Chub's idea. We Man Power guys were hang-

21

ing around the soft drink machine outside the Quick Shop just across from school drinking our Cokes. Chub took a swig and wiped his mouth against his sleeve as if he were wiping off beer suds like they do in TV commercials. "Ya know," he said, talking out of the side of his mouth, "ya drink beer and you won't have worms."

One thing led to another, and the first thing I knew I was aiding and abetting a robbery. Chub made off with a six-pack while the rest of us kept the attendant busy making change for a dollar. At the time it seemed like a joke. None of us would have even thought of it if it hadn't been for the thing at school. It wasn't until I got to college that I learned about reverse psychology.

We sneaked down the alley, Chub hiding the six-pack under his pullover sweater. "See." He snickered. "It said 'This Bud's for You!' Now we got to find a place to hide it. Chip, you live closest."

"Why me?" Not that Mom ever searched my room, but she always knew when something different was going on.

"Do you think I can carry it to my place? Ten blocks?" Chub slipped off his sweater and wrapped the loot into a less-suspicious-looking bundle.

"I know," Marv suggested. "Your mom's not home, Chip. Let's stash it in your garbage can. Tomorrow we can go down to the park. In the ravine."

"You mean drink it?" I asked. It was a dumb question.

"Sure." Chub looked at me as if I were the worm in the glass of beer. "You got to know what it tastes like so you'll know why you shouldn't drink it."

22

It made sense.

So we stuck the beer in our garbage can out by the alley. That night I put on a clean shirt before I came down to dinner.

"Would you pour the milk, Chip?" Mom said. "Then I think we're ready to eat."

I got out two glasses, set them on the counter, and opened the refrigerator door. Right there in front of the milk, was our six-pack of beer! I blinked, but it didn't go away. I glanced over at the wastepaper basket. It was empty. Of all times, Mom must have carried out the garbage herself instead of asking me. I waited for her to say something. She didn't.

Carefully I slid the six-pack over and pulled out the milk carton. It must have taken me five minutes to pour those glasses of milk. I had to wait until my ears quit burning. I put the milk back into the refrigerator in *front* of the six-pack and carried the glasses to the table.

"Thank you, Chip," Mom said without looking up.

The rest of the dinner was quiet—very quiet.

The next day the guys were really mad at me. "Where'd it go?"

"I didn't touch it!" I said. That was no lie.

"Dumb place to hide it anyway," Chub grumbled.

"Sure was," I agreed.

The six-pack took up space in our refrigerator for the next two months.

The next thing that happened just sneaked up on me, and I was in the middle before I knew what was going on.

"Now for the frosting on the cake," Mr. Hansen announced in our English class that day. "For the last four weeks of the year we're going to go spelunking. That's exploring caves, if you don't know the word."

Everyone sat up straighter and listened.

"We're going spelunking into . . ." he paused. "Spelunking into poetry."

The class groaned.

I didn't groan. Any other teacher would have called it a unit, which always sounded like something you had to swallow for your health. Nobody knew, not even Mom, that I liked poetry, that I had liked poetry ever since I'd read A. A. Milne and memorized, "They're changing the guard at Buckingham Palace, Christopher Robin went down with Alice."

"Here's what we're going to be doing for the first assignment."

For the rest of the class period I took notes, probably for the first time that semester. We were supposed to read about this place called Spoon River and how this guy, who lived just south of Chicago out in the country somewhere, visited a cemetery and then wrote a poem about each person who was buried where. We had to read a whole bunch of these poems and take a test over them and then we had to pick out our favorite and read it in front of the class.

This time it wasn't a groan. It was a howl of pain.

Mr. Hansen just folded his big arms and stood there smiling until everyone got quiet again.

"A little taste won't hurt you. If you don't like it, you can spit it out."

I thought of the six-pack of Bud still in our refrigerator.

It tasted good . . . very, very good—the poetry, but I

24

hid it from the guys just as I had hid the beer from Mom. I must have read that book of poems nine thousand times.

Somehow hearing Lucinda Matlock and Anne Rutledge and Fiddler Jones talking from their graves was like hearing my own father, whom I'd never even seen. One poem was about unknown soldiers. I read that one night late in my room and the awfulness of Vietnam hit me hard. It really did. That one line got me:

> . . . had we known what was back of their words
> We should not be lying here!

I even read about the man who wrote the poems: Edgar Lee Masters. Somehow, there wasn't so much time to hang around with the guys, and once I got started doing work for my English class, I started feeling guilty about history and math.

The first thing I knew, I was getting A's again, like nothing had ever happened, and I was doing the laundry for Mom and me every other time the way I used to, and taking showers, and I felt clean for the first time all year.

One afternoon Mom got home before I did, and when I walked in she grinned at me and handed me this big box. It was a really good-looking cotton sweater that I'd seen in a *New Yorker* ad. I'd never mentioned it to her, but it was like we were back in sync again and she had read my mind.

When I saw it, I knew it wasn't a bribe or a pay-off. It was just a present. For the first time in a long time, I grabbed her and hugged her and lifted her off the floor until she yanked at my ears and I had to put her down.

When I poured our milk that night, the six-pack of beer had disappeared.

I had chosen "The Hill" for my class presentation. Mr. Hansen creased open his grade book as he walked to the back of the classroom that day. "We'll start with you Mr. Prentiss. Let's hear how you and Edgar Lee Masters hit it off."

Chub looked over at Marv, rolled his eyes, squirmed farther down into his desk and muttered, "Didn't get it done. Didn't understand the assignment."

Mr. Hansen shrugged, made a mark in his grade book, and went on to Marv.

"Me neither," Marv echoed.

Mr. Hansen didn't bother to shrug. "Karen?" he went on.

Karen walked to the front of the room. I hadn't really noticed her much before, but now, standing up there, she looked different. She was one of those very pale blondes with skin to match—washed out—but now her cheeks were pink and she looked like a watercolor picture: delicate and really pretty, especially when she began to speak. She didn't have a book or notes or anything.

> "I went to the dances at Chandlerville,
> And played snap-out at Winchester."

Chub began to laugh. Karen went on as if she hadn't even heard him.

> "One time we changed partners,
> Driving home in the moonlight of middle June,
> And then I found Davis."

26

No one was laughing now, and when she came to the last lines she looked right at Chub and Marv.

> "Degenerate sons and daughters,
> Life is too strong for you—
> It takes life to love Life."

The class was quiet when she sat down. Karen had memorized the whole poem! She had become Lucinda Matlock, and we had heard her speaking from that Spoon River cemetery just as Edgar Lee Masters had.

Then it was my turn. I took the book with me, although I knew the poem by heart. Somehow I didn't want to spoil what Karen had done. Chub stuck out his foot and tried to trip me, but it didn't work.

There's something funny about standing up in front of a class. They were all the same kids as before, but they looked different, like a bunch of strangers. When you're sitting at a desk, you're one of the rest; when you stand in front, you're all alone.

I read the title of the poem, "The Hill," and Chub and Marv started snickering again, but quietly because Mr. Hansen was watching.

I stopped for a minute to think about the words I was going to read. Chub was making faces at me and Marv pretended to be falling asleep. They weren't funny. They weren't even original. I wondered how I'd ever spent so much time fooling around with them.

> "Where are Elmer, Herman, Beth,
> Tom, and Charley,
> The weak of will, the strong of arm,
> the clown, the boozer, the fighter?
> All, all, are sleeping on the hill."

27

As I went on, my voice got stronger. It didn't crack, and it didn't even sound like my voice. It was sort of like listening to a radio. By the time I got to the end of the poem, I had forgotten I was supposed to be reading, maybe because I was looking at Karen and she was smiling at me and looked as if she knew how much the words meant.

"They brought them dead sons from the war,
And daughters whom life had crushed,
And their children fatherless, crying."

When the class was over, Mr. Hansen stopped me by the door. "Good job, Chip," he said, as if I'd run for the winning touchdown.

Karen was waiting in the hall. It was the first time in my life a girl had ever waited for me, and I didn't know what to do. I didn't have to do anything. She looked at me the way Mom did sometimes when I carried out the garbage without being asked.

"You had yours memorized too, didn't you?" she asked as we walked down the hall together.

"Sort of," I answered, trying to match my stride to her steps. I wondered if she knew how hard it was when you had long legs to take little steps without stumbling.

"Are you going to try out for the play?"

"What play?"

"*Our Town.* You know, the Community Theatre's putting it on this summer and auditions begin as soon as school's out. I'll bet you could get a part. It's a lot like *Spoon River.*"

"Oh, yeah, sure. I haven't made up my mind yet." I hadn't even heard about it. When we got outside, she went one way and I went the other. Chub and Marv hadn't waited for me and I was glad. I liked walking home alone for a change.

Those last weeks of school I stopped being part of the MP's. That wasn't any big deal; I just sort of pulled out and it didn't take the guys long to catch on. I wondered if Abby noticed.

Since there wasn't anything else to do after school, I started running. The track was usually empty, and it was nice there by myself. It didn't take long to work up to an easy two miles, and I could sort of float along listening to my feet hit the cinders while my mind took its own direction.

I probably wouldn't have thought of the play again except for Mr. Hansen.

One afternoon, I was finishing the first lap and getting to that place where your whole body sort of becomes a machine and you forget about your legs and you're running without any effort, when I heard someone coming up behind me. Two guys passed me as if they were training for the Olympics—only they weren't guys, they were Mr. Hansen and Al Healey, the track coach at the high school. I didn't know him, but I'd seen his picture in the paper.

By the time I'd done two miles, they'd done three and weren't even winded.

Mr. Hansen called me over. They were a funny-looking pair. Hansen was short and thick and all muscle, Healey was taller than I, with muscles that you didn't notice unless he was running.

We jogged around, cooling off, talking about the condition of the track and how the high school baseball team was doing. It wasn't like they were teachers and I was a student. It was more like we were just three guys who were enjoying ourselves.

In the locker room, after we'd showered and were getting dressed, Mr. Hansen said, "Chip. You're going to try out for the play, aren't you?"

"I don't know," I said. "Never been in a play before. Don't even know what you have to do."

Hansen grinned, "Same thing you did with your poem the other day. Understand the words and share them with someone else."

Mr. Healey finished tying his sneakers and looked at me. "Yeah, Steve tells me you did a good job in his class last week."

I thought he must have been kidding, but he looked completely serious.

"Listen," he went on, "you'll be in high school next fall. Are you coming out for track?"

"Oh, come on, Al," Hansen broke in. "What are you doing? Recruiting?"

"Never thought about track," I said. "I don't know anything about running. I just do it."

"You do the same thing you were doing out there. Put one foot in front of the other and keep moving. Of course," Mr. Healey went on, "if you want to try it, I could show you a few basics. You'd have all summer to get in shape."

On the way home, I thought about Mr. Healey. I wasn't sure how old he was, but he was sure tall enough for Mom. Too bad Mr. Hansen was too short.

Chapter Three

*W*HEN I WAS FIFTEEN I fell in
love again. It lasted five minutes.
That whole summer was like one of Mom's casseroles:
I was never sure what was in it, but everything tasted
good. I ran every day, sometimes on the track and sometimes in the country outside of town. I'd see Healey
every week or so, and he'd make some suggestions about
my form. He even let me use the weight room at the
high school. Sometimes Pete ran with me, but most of
the time she was practicing with her summer league. Mr.
Hansen had me hooked, and I was working my way
through volumes of American poetry.

One evening I ran into Abby at the public library.
She was going in the revolving door as I was coming
out, so I just went right around again and caught up
with her.

"Hi." It was all I could think of to say. I was glad I wasn't wearing my ragged cut-offs.

She looked me up and down as if she were inspecting me.

"Do I pass?"

"It's a definite improvement."

"You noticed!"

"It'd be hard not to. Besides, Pete keeps me posted."

I could have hugged Pete.

"Hey. I haven't seen you around."

"Around what? The revolving door?"

At first I thought she was serious; then I saw this wicked little grin start up around the corner of her mouth. She was being funny. She was kidding me. She was human. She was Abby and she was talking to me!

"Look. I'll wait for you. We can walk home together."

The grin disappeared. "Thanks, but don't wait for me. My father's outside in the car."

She didn't say "good-by" or "nice seeing you" or "see you again" or anything. She just walked off.

I auditioned for the play and got the part of George Gibbs. Karen was Emily. Rehearsals didn't start until after the Fourth of July, but I had my lines memorized and most of the others too. Mom helped me a lot. I bet if she had tried, she could have been an actress. I hardly ever thought about Abby.

In June, Mom and I went to Colorado. Mom loved the mountains. We had a time-share condo there. That's the only place we ever went for vacation, once in the spring and once in the winter. As usual, we saw Mom's old friend, Jake, the ex-judge, and his wife. They lived there year round. Rob and his folks were there too. Rob and I had talked to each other on the phone about once a month, so when we saw each other, it was like nothing had changed.

Something did change when I got home and rehearsals started. Karen and I began to spend most of our spare time together. At first we just practiced our lines, but pretty soon we began talking to each other, really talking, about things that mattered and about what it was like to be growing up in Collinsville.

One evening we were in the park, sitting on the swings where Pete had run into me—backwards. It was the week before the play opened. We'd been talking about what it would actually be like when we got up on stage in front of people.

Karen looked at me, started to say something, and stopped and blushed. I couldn't believe how pretty it looked when she did it, and how awful it felt when it was me.

"Something wrong?" I asked.

"I brought you a present . . . for good luck. It isn't much. I hope you like it."

She pulled a book out of the backpack she always carried and handed it to me. It was a book I'd never seen before: *Winesburg, Ohio* by Sherwood Anderson. I flipped open the first page and read the dedication. "To the memory of my mother . . . who first awoke in me the hunger to see beneath the surface of lives." I looked at Karen.

"I read it first—before I gave it to you. Hope you don't mind. I marked one story for you to read. It's called 'Sophistication'."

I still have the book. Only it's Abby I think about when I read it.

The week the play went into production, Karen was the only one in my mind. When you're on stage with just one person, she can either make your scene or goof it up, so you have to depend on her, and a funny thing happened. Somehow the characters we were being, Emily and George, sort of melted into who we really were. The illusion we were creating on the stage filtered into the hours of our being Chip and Karen, and when I kissed her, in Act I, it was like kissing two people at once, or maybe like four people kissing each other all at the same time. I was confused. It was a good thing Karen wasn't.

The playhouse was sold out the last night, and you know how it is when you're up on stage: all you can see out there in the audience is a mass of floating heads. Mom was there, of course. She came all five nights. It was Karen's and my big scene, and I looked across the stage and it was as if she were caught in a bubble of light and all sorts of sparkly things were radiating from her. A shiver went all through me, and I almost forgot my next line. I felt suddenly clean and empty from the inside out. I loved her. If it's ever happened to you, I don't need to describe it, and if it hasn't, there's no way I could. Karen's lines came out as if she were actually asking me . . . me, Chip Martin, "If you love me, help me. All I want is someone to love me."

"I will, Emily. Emily, I'll try," I replied on cue, but they were *my* words.

The curtain finally came down. The house lights went up. Karen reached for my hand, but before we could run out to take our bows, I grabbed her in my arms and kissed her . . . really kissed her.

Standing on the apron, blinking into the house lights, it occurred to me that Karen hadn't kissed me back.

34

There wasn't time to think about it then because the whole cast was out front and the audience was standing up applauding. I saw Pete grinning up at me. Abby was beside her, but she wasn't clapping; she wasn't doing anything. It was as if she'd sent her body to the play while the rest of her was somewhere else. There wasn't time to think about that either.

At the cast party, everybody was laughing and shouting and congratulating each other. It should have been fun, but there was something sad about it too, because the Mrs. Evans and the Emily and the George were gone, and we were all just ourselves again. Karen was only Karen; the radiance had disappeared, and my moment of love had evaporated.

We walked home together, Karen and I. We held hands as we turned into the park, but there wasn't any magic between us, only a kind of warmth. It wasn't exciting, it was comfortable.

I was just going to ask her if she was feeling what I felt when I saw Abby and her dad sitting on one of the benches at the edge of the park. They weren't talking or anything, just sitting there enjoying the evening together, his arm draped along the back of the bench, and Abby bending forward, her elbows on her knees. It was kind of like a Norman Rockwell cover on one of those old *Saturday Evening Posts*—a portrait of a father and daughter.

"Hi, Abby," Karen said tugging me toward the bench. "Did you like the play? Hello, Dr. Morris. You know Chip Martin, don't you?"

He didn't, of course, though we'd seen each other around, so we went through the whole handshaking thing. He was a tall, well-built man: broad shoulders,

35

clean-cut. Just the kind of man I always imagined my own father would have been.

"You both did a fine job, tonight," he said. "We put on the same play when I was in high school. I was the stage manager."

"You probably could have been our prompter." Karen laughed. "Could you still remember some of the lines?"

"Yes, I could. There's something about memorizing that makes it your own. You know, I wanted Abigail to try out for the play, but . . ."

"I'm not very good at acting, Dad. You know that," Abby said, as if it were a secret between them.

"You'd be good, Abby," Karen went on.

"You would, you know. Really," I repeated, feeling like a gawky George Gibbs reading his lines for the first time.

We talked for a while, stuff about school and about Pete's athletic career. Abby didn't say much, but she didn't have to; Karen and Dr. Morris rattled away as if they were old friends.

Finally, Abby stood up and looked at her watch. "Dad, we'd better go. It's getting late and Mom might be worried."

Just for a second she sounded as if she were the mother and he was a little kid. Then she laughed. "Mom's a runner, and she knows exactly how long it takes to get anywhere."

"Right!" he said, putting his hand on her sleeve. "Abigail and I are strollers. It was nice meeting you, Chip. I've heard a lot about you from Pete. Come over some time. And you too, Karen."

"We will," Karen answered for both of us.

Abby looked at me as if she wanted to say something,

but then she and her father walked down the street one way, and we went the other.

"You know, Abby's father was right," Karen said. "She should have tried out for a part. Not that I don't like her, but . . . she's not quite real."

"How about you?" I asked, trying to steer the conversation away from Abby. "You going to go on with acting? It's really important to you, isn't it?"

The rest of the way home Karen talked about how it felt to her to be on stage and what she wanted to do after high school and college. She had her life all planned out, and by the time we got to her front door, I was pretty well convinced she'd do exactly what she wanted.

Mom was waiting up for me when I got home. "How does it feel to 'tread the boards' and play to a standing-room-only-house?"

"Scary," I said, falling into the easy chair. "Sort of let down, now that it's over."

"The fleeting glow of fame," she moaned dramatically. "Are Karen's feet on the ground yet? She really was wonderful. And you were too, of course."

"She wants to be an actress, Mom. I mean really. For me, acting is kind of like the play says about life: awful, but wonderful, and when it's over, it's over—gone—and there's not much of anything left."

"Oh, but school starts next week. You'll have your track. You have a new friend in Karen. Nothing's over. It's just beginning."

"But what if he's right? Thornton Wilder, I mean, in the play. What if living is just a kind of kid's game, like Blind Man's Buff?" The idea had been nudging around in the back of my mind ever since I'd first read the script.

Mom didn't answer right away. She was good at knowing when I was being serious. Then she walked over to me and bent down, resting her cheek against my hair. Mom always smelled so beautiful—sort of like leaves on a fall afternoon. "I don't know the Blind Man's Buff part. I don't *think* that's the way it is. If there is any secret about living, maybe that's it—always reaching for where you're going, even if you don't know where you're headed."

Chapter Four

I LEARNED in kindergarten, and kept learning in every grade after, that the first day of classes was like being in the middle of a clothes dryer set on spin. High school was no different. The building was twice as large as our old junior high, and I got lost three times trying to find my way around. I was certain I'd never make it through to graduation.

My last class of the day was English. Any class, last hour, is a bummer, but last-hour English is a lost cause, and to make it even worse, Mr. Kruger, who looked as if he'd already given up on us, announced alphabetically assigned seats.

"Martin," he barked.

I sat down next to some guy named Larson.

"Morris."

I looked up and there was Abby standing by the door hugging a notebook.

"What are you doing here?" I whispered as she sat down across the aisle from me.

"I was put in an advanced section. I come here for English."

I was about to answer, "How come?", but I swallowed and thought the words instead. An eighth grader in a ninth grade class! She'd probably stay up all night studying and raise the curve, and Mr. Kruger looked as if he were going to be one of those lay-on-the-homework kind.

Abby edged her desk away so there was a wider aisle between us and flipped open her notebook.

"What's the matter? Think I'm going to copy?"

She looked at me, then glanced away without answering.

As soon as the bell rang for classes to begin, Mr. Kruger jumped into the grammar text like a diver after pearls and came up with a week's work on dangling modifiers.

Abby bent over her notebook as if she were recording every word; then she shifted the page so I could read.

"Dangling modifiers are obscene."

I tried not to laugh, and when Mr. Kruger was busy writing something on the board, I scrawled back, "If you think danglers are obscene, what about split infinitives?"

Kruger turned around to the class. Abby waited, then wrote, "How about vowel sounds?"

"Or colons," I whispered.

It was juvenile, I knew, but it was the first time I had seen Abby giggle. Almost every time I had ever seen her, she'd been so serious, as if she were thinking about things that were more important than what was going on around her.

"You all understand now what modifiers are?" Mr. Kruger looked right at Abby and me. We nodded, and he slid into participles.

I looked out the window. Grammar was not only obscene, it was boring. The September sky was so blue—that intense blue that makes you ache inside, and I got thinking about modifiers. They lived hidden away, I decided, gray slimy things like leeches, spending all their time multiplying until harvest time, when English teachers dug them up and stuffed them between the pages of grammar textbooks. Like leeches, modifiers sucked, and we were going to have to live with them for a whole week. I was going to write all that in a note to Abby, but I decided it sounded too dirty. After all, she was only in eighth grade.

When class ended, I walked partway down the hall with her, as far as my locker. "How does it feel to be in two places at once?" I asked. She looked so surprised that I hurried to add, "I mean two schools at the same time?"

"Oh, you'd be surprised how easy it is. All it takes is practice." Then she giggled. "Don't trip over any dangling modifiers. See you tomorrow." She hurried down the hall without looking back. I stood, one hand on the cold metal of my locker door, and watched her leave.

The last class of the day gradually became the most important class of the day, mostly because I shared it with Abby. I undangled participles, splinted infinitives, and mended sentence fragments until I wondered if there was a place in the world for verbal surgeons. The language I'd spoken all my life became an obstacle course as fascinating as the ones I followed when I ran.

And I did run. Every night after school, every weekend. Of course there was no chance of my making the cross-country team that fall, but Coach Healey kind of hinted that I should try out next year. I ran through the park, through the golf course and up and down the hills. I always ran alone, mostly because I liked it better that way. When I was alone, I wasn't competing against anybody but myself.

One crisp afternoon in the middle of October, I was pounding my way up the road to the top of Fowler's Hill just outside of town. The road was seldom used, but it was beautiful, with oak and maple trees arched above. I must have slowed down to kind of soak in the sky and the colors when I heard someone behind me.

Steps slowed to match mine.

"Hi. Okay if I run with you?"

It was Abby's mother, dressed in a blue Vortex jogging suit that must have fractured a couple of hundred dollar bills.

"Sure. If I can keep up."

"No race, you know. I'm Peg Morris."

"I know. I've seen you go by our house. I'm Chip Martin."

"Of course. Pete's friend. She talks about you all the time. You and Abby are in the same English class, I hear."

We jogged on up to the top of the hill. I had intended to stop, but it was Abby's mother who suggested it. "I usually give myself a break about here. There's something about the crest of a hill that sort of catches your breath."

"Yeah, I know. Power, maybe."

"Or maybe it's because you can see everything at once and everything's in its right place."

"Yeah." It wasn't like talking to Mom, but it was easier than talking to Abby. I didn't want to stare at her, but I kept looking for something in her face that was like Pete or Abby. She had reddish hair and her eyes were dark, but beyond that she could have been anybody. One thing for sure, she was in good shape. She wasn't even breathing hard.

"Do you run up here often?" I tried to sound adult.

"Only when the weather's nice." She jogged in place, relaxing and twisting her arms. "I get tired of pounding sidewalks." She half laughed. "Good thing running is socially acceptable, or my husband would be out of business."

"Why?" I couldn't see the connection.

"Professional men, so they tell me, are successful in proportion to how properly their wives behave."

I wanted to laugh. I could just hear what Mom would have said to that comment. Instead I said, as seriously as I could, "I guess you have to be careful if you're a dentist."

"You got it." She laughed. "You never know what might come out of a patient's mouth besides teeth."

She sounded like Abby then, and I liked her.

"Are you on the track team?" She looked directly at me for the first time.

"No. Not yet. But I'm going to try out cross-country. I don't like running around in circles—and I always figured if I had to pass a baton, I'd drop it. Besides, I've got more endurance than speed."

"You sound like me. I guess the only bad thing about running is that the only thing you can do is think, at least until you hit that . . . you know."

"Yeah. That second breath."

"The high," she said.

"I know. When I first started running, I even counted the times my feet hit the ground."

Abby's mother laughed. "I went through the alphabet."

"Not any more?" I asked.

"Nope. Now I just let the wind whistle through my ears. It clears the head."

We turned and started back down the hill, running a smooth easy pace side by side as if we were hooked together by some invisible wire. As I turned up the sidewalk to our front door, she called, "Want to do this again? Say next week, about the same time?"

While I showered and changed clothes, I decided it really would be fun. Maybe it would be kind of like having a grown-up Pete around—or an Abby.

The next Monday, I followed Abby out of English class—not on purpose really. She usually grabbed up her books as soon as the last bell rang and was out of the room before I could untangle my legs and move, but this time Mr. Kruger caught her—something about her last paper, I guess—so that after I'd gone to my locker for my coat, she was hurrying down the hall.

"Hey. Hold up. I'll walk with you," I shouted

She half turned but kept on walking.

"Abby!" I hurried to catch up to her. "You going home?"

"Yes. Mother's at her aerobic class and I have to get home so Pete won't be alone."

I held the door open for her, and we started down the walk.

"Thought you ran every night."

"Usually do."

"Mother says you've been running around with her."

At first I hoped she was jealous, and then I figured out she was making a joke.

"She's a neat lady."

"Mother is . . ." She paused as if she were choosing her words. "My mother is happiest when she's doing something."

"She doesn't have a job? I mean besides taking care of the house and all?"

"No. She does aerobics and swims. She used to read a lot. Now she runs instead."

"Well, I do have a job. Mom said I had to rake leaves. The neighbors have theirs raked, and she said they'd run us out of the neighborhood if our leaves started blowing all over their lawns. I don't mind though."

"People shouldn't pick up leaves. I like them lying underneath a tree just the way they fell."

The sidewalk was wide and I wondered what she'd do when it narrowed down, because she was walking clear over on one edge, as far away from me as she could get.

"When I was little, I used to go out and cover myself up with leaves so that no one could find me. Once my father thought I was lost, and he looked all over for me, shouting like mad, and I just lay there under the pile of leaves and didn't answer. I was little then. I didn't do it again."

"What did he do? Paddle you?"

45

"No." She balanced on the edge of the walk putting each foot in the front of the other as if she were on a tightrope. "He gave me a ten-minute lecture on how I should never hide from him again. But I still like piles of leaves. They smell so pretty and they crunch so nicely."

I moved over to the middle of the walk.

With some girls you have to worry about what to say next so they won't think you're stupid, and you have trouble listening because you're so busy thinking up what you're going to say next. Today with Abby, there was no problem. It was like throwing a stone in the water and watching the ripples spread.

"I like the smell of burning leaves," I said, moving back over to my side of the walk.

"Did you know you can smell the colors when they burn? Reds smell sweet. Browns and yellows burn your nose. I've never figured out why." She moved over toward the middle of the walk, keeping two steps ahead of me.

"Who said colors smell?" I didn't know why, but I felt I had to challenge her—maybe I only wanted to tease her.

"Nobody *said*. I *know*. Pink smells ucky. Gray smells dirty. Black smells fresh. You can taste colors. Hear them, too. I can even close my eyes and see colors. Can you?"

"Never tried." I felt as if I were dunked under water and allowed to come up just in time to take another breath and then pushed down again.

"I dream in color. Do you?" She didn't wait for my answer. "Sometimes I can even decide before I go to sleep what I'm going to dream about. And I do. I can decide I'm going to fly, and then I go to sleep and zoom out my window and fly anywhere I want to. Most of the time I don't go too high—just skim over the tops of trees."

"You've read too much Peter Pan," I said trying to be clever.

Abby stopped and turned around, her mouth sort of tight around the edges. "You're making fun of me. Don't you believe me?"

"No, honest! I was just kidding. I believe you." I felt dizzy.

"Don't ever laugh at me!" We were almost to her house. I walked up beside her, and my coat sleeve brushed against her arm. She jerked away from me and ran down the street and into her house without another word.

I stood like a stupe and watched her go. I had no idea what I had done. I tried to think what I had said. At first I felt like punching someone. One thing I knew, girls were different, and I wasn't sure I ever wanted to see one again—at least not one like Abby.

The next day in class, Mr. Kruger had us reading "To a Waterfowl" by some old man who looked as if a whole flock of fowls could have made a comfortable nest in his beard.

He who, from zone to zone,
Guides through the boundless sky thy certain flight,
In the long way . . .

Mr. Kruger insisted poetry should be read aloud just the way songs should be sung aloud. It made sense, and I was really trying to listen until Abby passed me a note. She had come in late, slipped into the desk next to mine without saying a word, opened up her book, and started to read.

"What does a water fowl look like?" the note said.

I scribbled back, "Don't know. It smells though. Foul!"

So we sat and drew pictures of birds with appropriate names. "A small snit sitting on the horns of a dilemma." That was Abby's. I drew a "large huff" and a "little spat." Abby giggled. Mr. Kruger frowned.

I was definitely in love.

After fall track, the weather turned cold, and then it was Thanksgiving and tests and a new semester. Abby aced the English class, both semesters. I ace-minused it. I could have done better if I'd paid more attention to Mr. Kruger and less to Abby, but in class, at least, she was always there tugging at the corner of my mind. I had never figured out what had happened on our walk home that night.

Chapter Five

*T*HE NEXT YEAR, the Abby in high school was not the same as the Abby in junior high. It was as if a secret button had been pressed and she exploded into action. She volunteered for everything. She was a newspaper reporter, squad leader in her gym class, and on the honor roll. She had meetings every morning before school, and she never left until after five.

"What are you? Some sort of workaholic?" I asked her one day. It was a Saturday in early fall, and I was picking up a little pocket money raking lawns. We sat down on my newly raked pile of leaves. I hadn't seen much of her since our English class the year before. She looked at me with that blank way of hers that made you feel not only she was disappearing, but you were too, and said,

"No. I'm a schoolaholic. I like school. It's one place I don't have to think."

"What do you mean you don't have to think?"

"Just that. Like algebra. You just do it as the teacher tells you, and you don't have to think about anything else. If I'm reading, I can't hear the stereo or TV or anything. You can look at one thing, too, and not see anything else around. I read in a book once that if you were really good at concentrating you could move right out of your body and go someplace else."

"It's called psychokinesis. It's not scientific though."

"You sound like Mr. Kruger and his poetry. There's only one right way and it's his. That's what I mean. You don't have to think in school. They tell you how, only it's never about things that matter."

I picked up a leaf and twirled it between my fingers. It was easy to talk to Abby, but I was always afraid I might say the one wrong thing that would suddenly turn her into a somebody I didn't know. I wanted to ask her what did matter, but instead I said, "Maybe we should try."

"Try what?" She sat up as if she were going to run.

"Psychokinesis. See. I'm going to have my body stay here and I'm going to fly right over to our kitchen and pop myself a Coke."

"That isn't the way you do it."

"Quiet," I warned her. "I'm concentrating."

I closed my eyes and tried to imagine myself jogging off down the street, turning into our drive, opening the kitchen door, and rushing over to the refrigerator, but I couldn't. All I could think of was Abby there beside me. Even with my eyes closed, I could see her, smell her, feel her. She had changed over the summer—matured, somehow—softened really. I felt a terrible urge to touch her . . . to brush my fingers against her arm, to cup her chin in one hand and feel the velvet of her throat.

Instead, I hauled myself to my feet and stood looking down at her. I felt warm all over, as if I really had left my body and jogged all the way home, and yet there was a strange rightness about the feeling, as if this were the way it was supposed to be.

"I don't believe you were thinking about Coke," Abby said, with a private little smile.

"How did you know?" I was blushing now.

"There's something called mental telepathy too. That was in the same book." She looked up at me. There was no shadow in her eyes.

I saw Abby's face change again even before I heard the footsteps.

"Well, what's going on here?" His voice was soft.

Abby stood up and brushed the leaves from her skirt. "I was trying to get Chip to buy some tickets for the school party. Everybody on Student Council has to sell ten tickets and I only have these two left." She reached into her pocket.

Abby's father watched her. Not once did he look at me.

"I'll take them, I'll take them." I said, trying to keep my voice from jumping two octaves. "After I collect my money for this lawn." I wondered why we were lying.

Dr. Morris still did not look at me. He stood watching her. She might have been some sort of goddess springing to life from the fallen leaves; at least, at that minute, that's the way she looked to me. Then, as if he suddenly remembered I was there, he turned. "I suppose you know my Abigail has taken over the running of Collins-

51

ville High this year." He laughed a deep chuckle and rested his arm across Abby's shoulders. "She's a charmer, my Abigail. Isn't she?"

"Oh, Dad." Abby twisted away from him and handed me the tickets. "You can pay me later."

"Pete tells me you're on the cross-country team this year." Dr. Morris looked me up and down as if he were calculating my weight and height.

"Well, not exactly yet," I tried to explain. "There are two guys ahead of me, but the coach thinks I might make it. Were you a track man?"

"Oh no, not me." He laughed, but he looked kind of pleased as if I'd given him a compliment. "My wife's the physical fitness freak—jogging, aerobics, exercises, all of that. Always has been. Pete takes after her mother; Abigail is mine."

"Well, it takes all kinds." That had to be the dumbest thing I'd ever said, but he didn't seem to notice because he laughed again as if he'd never heard the words before.

"Chip, it's good to see you again. Stop over sometime when you're not busy. You and my wife can talk about running shoes." He turned back to Abby. "Come on honey, you've sold your tickets. House-cleaning time."

Abby was standing there, her hands shoved deep in her pockets, scuffing at the leaves. She didn't answer.

Dr. Morris smiled at me again and put a hand on my shoulder. "Saturdays my wife and Pete are out being athletic. Abigail and I do the weekend chores. But any other time, Chip—come on over."

Then they were gone, and I was standing there with two tickets in my hand. Abby's dad was a really nice guy. He seemed to like me. It all linked together like an equation. I'd stop at their house the next afternoon and pay for the tickets. I'd ask Abby to go to the party with me. It would be our first real date.

That night, I sat up in my room trying to decide how to ask Abby. "Here's the money for those two tickets. Want to go with me?" That sounded sort of spur-of-the moment, as if it had just occurred to me to ask. "Abby, can I take you to the party?" "Want me to come around and pick you up? I've got two tickets." "How about going to the party with me?" "Do you suppose we could go to the party together?" The thing about putting it into a question was that she might say no.

"I've got two tickets. I'll take you to the party." That sounded sort of pushy. "Let's go to the party together." "I'll stop by for you and we can go together." That sounded too casual.

Maybe I'd just go over and pay for the tickets and call when I got back home. That way, if she said no, I could hang up. Of course, I could wait until I saw her at school. "How's the party coming? Maybe. . . ."

I finally gave up and went downstairs. Mom was at her desk tapping out some business figures on her computer. I hated to interrupt her, but she finally saw me standing there.

"Something wrong?"

I guess all parents are alike. When you really want to know about something, the first conclusion they jump to is that something is wrong.

"Nothing," I mumbled. "Just thinking."

"Fine!" Mom kidded. "Nobody ever went wrong thinking."

"I mean, I was thinking, maybe, about asking Abby to go to the school party. She pawned two tickets off on me."

"Why didn't you ask her then?"

"Her dad was there. But I haven't paid for them yet, so I sort of thought I'd go over tomorrow and pay for them and ask her."

"Sounds fine to me."

"Yeah." I slumped down into a chair. "But Mom. It's this way. What if she says no? I mean, how can I ask her so she won't say no?"

"Good night! What's the matter with you? You've known Abby for how long now? Three, four years? You just ask her. 'Hey, want to go to the party with me?' "

"Oh, Mom. I can't do that. How did Dad ask . . . the first time?"

"Chip, that was so long ago. I can't even remember. Maybe I asked him."

"You asked him!"

"Maybe. I can't remember. Listen, Chip, there are some things in life you can't plan for. You don't sit down and write a script. You play it by ear. Like with Abby. You're friends. Good friends, I imagine, and when you go over to pay for the tickets, and you're talking together, there'll be a chance for you to ask her—just casually and naturally."

But Mom didn't know. There was nothing casual about Abby. She wasn't just any girl. She was Abby, and there were so many things I didn't understand about her: so warm one time and then next day icily cool.

I waited until the middle of the afternoon to go to Abby's. I was sure her family would have a proper Sunday dinner, at one or two o'clock.

Abby answered the door and led me into the living room, and it was the funniest thing. All I could think of was that old film I'd seen on TV about when they first tested the atomic bomb out in that desert, and they had a house all set up with a dummy mother and father and children sitting around, waiting for the bomb to go off.

"Hello, Chip." Dr. Morris stood up and shook my hand as if he were making plans to sell me a new set of teeth.

"Nice to see you, Chip." Mrs. Morris turned down the stereo. Pete, sprawled out on her stomach reading the sports page, merely lifted her head and said, "Hi," as if it were perfectly natural for me to come over on a Sunday afternoon.

Dr. Morris sat down. Abby sat down. Mrs. Morris sat down, and there I was standing in the middle of the room. The only vacant spot left was a love seat by Mrs. Morris. I shuffled over and sat down too. The thing was covered with some silky material and I almost slid off. I had the feeling no one ever sat on it. It was hard, and the wood on the back caught me right between the shoulder blades, and it was so low I had to peer between my knees to see.

"Glad you stopped in. Most of the time it's like living in a harem around here." Dr. Morris chuckled at his own words.

"How's your mother?" Mrs. Morris ventured.

"Fine."

"I've never met your father, though. What does he do?"

"I don't have a father."

Dr. Morris looked up.

Mrs. Morris' eyebrows flew up. Abby laughed.

"What I mean is, I never knew my father. He was in the Air Force. Vietnam."

"You mean he was killed? Your mother never re-married?"

"Missing in action. He still is. I guess Mom still thinks he's alive."

"A noble sacrifice," Dr. Morris said as if he were going to make a speech, but he picked up his paper instead. "Unfortunately, I was in dentistry school."

"Your father. Was he drafted?" Abby's mother wasn't anything like the Peg Morris I jogged with.

"No, volunteered. See, he and Mom were mixed up in all those anti-war demonstrations, until my father decided he'd better see what he was demonstrating against. Guess he thought he could do something about stopping the war from the inside out."

"And your mother has her own business?"

Dr. Morris lifted his head again. "It must be difficult to grow up without a father."

That was the way it went: Mrs. Morris asking questions, Dr. Morris making statements, and Abby saying nothing. The only natural thing in the room was Pete, flipping the pages and drumming her toes on the floor.

After about half an hour, I struggled up from the love seat with, "Well, it's been nice but I think I'd better get home. I have to pay you for the tickets, Abby."

"Come again, any time, Chip?" Mrs. Morris said making it sound like a question.

"Abigail," Dr. Morris said, and it wasn't a question. "Show Chip the door."

Abby walked with me down the hall and stopped suddenly, then pointed dramatically. "That, Chip, is the door! See, I'm showing it to you."

We got outside before we started laughing.

"Does he always talk like that?" I asked.

"Always." Abby laughed again. "And I think you passed Mother's multiple choice exam."

We sat down on the front steps and I handed her the money for the tickets.

"Look," I said, "I'm a lousy dancer, but how about coming to the party with me? Maybe we could sit and draw birds, dangle some modifiers, or something." I hadn't realize until the words were out how much I really *did* want Abby to say yes.

She didn't. The laughter faded from her face and she started staring at the sidewalk as if she were studying for one of Mr. Kruger's grammar tests.

"That's nice of you, but . . ." She must not have seen the answer on the sidewalk because she started fooling with her watch. "Well, I have to be there early, and I promised to stay and clean up afterwards."

It wasn't as awful as it might have been. At least she hadn't just said no. We both stood up. Then she started talking again in a voice I'd never heard before, sort of tight and hard and breathless all at once.

Dr. Morris was standing in the doorway.

"Sure, Chip. I'd love to go with you, if you don't mind being there ahead of everyone else. Maybe you'd even help me set up the tables."

She didn't wait for an answer. Her father held the door open for her. I waved to both of them and headed for home. I don't think my feet even touched the sidewalk. Abby was mine, at least for one evening. I didn't bother to question why Abby had changed her mind.

Chapter Six

GETTING READY for my date with Abby was almost as hard as asking her in the first place.

About the middle of the afternoon, I thought I'd better lay out my clothes. Of course, I didn't have to pick up Abby until six-thirty and it was only two, but Mom was working at her office, so I knew I'd have the bathroom as long as I wanted and plenty of hot water.

I don't know if girls do it, but when I opened my closet door, I couldn't find a thing to wear. There was all the stuff I wore to school, but that wouldn't do—Abby had seen everything. Of course, there were my madras jacket and white pants, but this was October. That left my new cords, but they were brown and my best sweater was blue. There was the rust pullover Aunt Millie had sent me, but it had that idiotic alligator on the front. It took me about a half-hour, a razor blade, and Mom's tweezers to dissect the amphibian and peel it off. I didn't think the little holes would show in the dark. Then there were shoes. Adidas were out. Loafers looked too casual. I settled for my boots. It took a good hour and a fourth bottle of neat's-foot oil before I got them polished the way I wanted them.

By four-thirty I headed for the shower.

I was out of shampoo so I borrowed Mom's. I borrowed her razor too, just in case. My can of deodorant was empty, so I used Mom's, but I decided between her shampoo and her deodorant, I smelled like an English country garden—lavender, lilacs, and lilies—and that wasn't the kind of image I wanted to project. So I got back into the shower and washed all the sweetness away.

I headed back to my bedroom and looked over the collection of colognes I had amassed from the last two Christmases: Macho? Brut? They were too powerful. Charisma? I liked the name but it smelled like the hot lunch room at school. English Leather. That was it. It sort of matched my boots. I poured out a good handful and figured it could take the place of the deodorant I didn't have. I dabbed the stuff over my chest too and across my shoulders and finally dumped the rest of the bottle over my head. Even my second shower hadn't squelched the smell of Mom's shampoo.

I was sitting in the kitchen, all dressed, staring at the clock when Mom came home. She walked in the door, took a deep breath, and backed out. A moment later she opened the door again, just enough to poke her head through and said, "Good grief! It smells like a saddle factory in here."

"Too much?" I asked. By that time I couldn't smell anything.

She closed the door behind her and leaned back. "Well," she said slowly, "Just a little. But if you stay outside and walk fast, it may wear off. Or maybe we could turn a fan on."

"Is it that bad?" I sniffed under each arm.

"Chip, it's a cliché, I know, but less is always more— including English Leather."

She looked up at the clock. "Six-thirty, you say?"

"Yes."

"Go take another shower. I think you've built up a reserve that will last the evening."

At 6:26 I whistled my way to Abby's. I was either happy or scared. I think I was both. She was coming down the steps when I got there. I wanted to think she'd been watching for me.

"Hope you don't mind walking," I said, trying not to stare at her. She was the same, only different, and I couldn't figure out why. Her face was sort of flushed, and I was pretty sure it wasn't make-up, and her smile was a little bit too wide to be real.

"Why would I mind walking? I walk it every day." Then she turned toward me, her face relaxed now. "You sure smell good!"

"So do you." To tell the truth I still couldn't smell anything, but one thing I knew for sure, Abby *looked* good.

Then our conversation stopped flat. It was another block before I could think of anything to say and then it was stupid: "Do you know you're the first date I've ever had, and all of a sudden I don't know how to talk."

"Well, Chip," she said with that adult tone in her

60

voice. "You don't *have* me." Then the laughter crept into her voice. "Isn't it dumb? Maybe we should think of a list of topics we could talk about, like Mr. Kruger taught us in English."

After that it was easy. All the way to school we listed all the topics we could think of from aardvarks to ziggurats. It was so simple and wonderful—the joy of making Abby laugh.

We went on laughing the rest of the evening. First Abby had me shoving tables and carrying chairs, so by the time everyone else came, I was dripping with sweat and in dire need of a fourth shower.

We laughed hardest at our one attempt at dancing. Just when our steps were about matching the music, my boots would skid. I must have got neat's-foot oil on the bottoms. We finally gave up.

"I may be a lousy dancer, but I'm really a pretty good skater," I said as we headed for the punchbowl—grape Kool-Aid with half-melted ice cubes floating around like protoplasm.

"Next time, we'll have the party at the hockey rink."

Abby had said, "Next time." The grape Kool-Aid slipped down my throat like champagne.

We never did get around to talking about aardvarks or ziggurats. Somehow there wasn't time. Abby stood at the table and poured grape Kool-Aid into spongy plastic cups, and I filled flimsy paper plates full of Home Economic cookies. That may not sound like fun, but I'd look up and see Abby looking back at me, and we'd both smile—not grin, smile—and there's a big difference.

It must have been around ten-thirty. The party was over, stuff was cleaned up. Everyone had left, and Abby and I were heading for the gym door. The custodian flipped off the lights and the gym was dark except for the exit light. There was something eerie about the place. One minute it had been full of music and people and noise, and now all we could hear were our footsteps. It was like being caught in a time warp or off in a black hole in space.

"You'll never find me." I heard Abby's laugh somewhere behind me.

"Keep talking," I said, turning around and groping in the dark. I felt her run past. I reached out and grabbed. I didn't hurt her. I barely touched her. She didn't scream or yell or anything, but she made this awful low muffled sound as if she were going to be sick or something.

Before I could say anything, my feet went out from under me and I landed flat on my back, my head bouncing on the hard wood floor of the gym.

Then Abby was kneeling beside me, sort of crying, I think. I'm sure I felt a tear on my hand.

"I'm sorry," Abby whispered, her voice low and husky. "It was like the beginning of a nightmare."

The lights flashed back on, and walking toward us across the length of the gym was Abby's father. I stumbled to my feet and pulled Abby up with me. She held my hand as if she were still caught in her bad dream.

"I've been waiting for you, Abigail. I got worried."

"What were you waiting for?" Abby said in a voice that was different again.

"You and Chip. I didn't want you walking home alone in the dark." He turned to me. "I know you're perfectly capable of taking care of Abigail, Chip, but you know how fathers are."

I didn't.

Abby let go of my hand.

That's how my first date with Abby ended. She huddled in the corner of the back seat. I sat in front with her father as we drove the ten blocks back to *my* front door.

"You caught a ride home?" Mom said in that tell-me-all-about-it tone that mothers sometimes use.

"Yeah! Abby's father drove us home."

"Her father!"

Mom flipped her magazine page and pretended she was reading, but she was trying not to laugh.

"Her father!" I repeated sitting down on the sofa and pulling off my boots. "You know, Mom. I'm glad I don't have a father. I can tell you one thing. If I ever do have a kid of my own, you won't see me hanging around when she has a date."

"Well, Chip." Mom closed her magazine. "There are fathers and then there are fathers. Of course, mine never did that to me. I suppose it was Abby's first date too."

"I suppose." My feet hurt. For all the dancing I had done, I could have worn my Adidas.

"Look at it this way, Chip. Abby's lucky to have a father who cares that much."

"Sure," I said, but I wasn't *sure*.

That was the first and last real date I had with Abby that year. Of course, she was only fifteen. I was sixteen, and I was in love. We were together often, but we were never together alone.

That winter I got used to picking Abby up and walking her to all the basketball games and stuff and riding home in the front seat with her father—a silent Abby scrunched up in the back seat.

I did ask her out once. It was a Friday night and there was a movie in town we both wanted to see. We were walking home from school. We always took the long way, past Pete's elementary school, and if Pete was around, she'd walk with us.

"Well, would you like to? I'll even buy the tickets." It was snowing, I remember. Abby was wearing a fuzzy red hat, and the snowflakes stuck to it and melted. I remember thinking how very pretty she was and how I wanted to tell her so.

"I'd like to Chip, but I can't. Not on Friday night."

"How come? Does your father have you chained to the kitchen sink?"

"No." Abby frowned. "I have to clean the house."

"I thought you did that Saturday morning."

"Not any more. Pete's taking swimming lessons at the Y."

"What's that got to do with anything?"

"Father runs an organized household. He doesn't go to the office on Saturdays, so it's Mom's time off. He takes care of Pete and me, and Mom goes shopping or meets some of her friends downtown for lunch. It's been that way as long as I can remember."

"And you and your Dad and Pete clean house?"

"Not any more. I've decided it's our morning out, too—for Pete and me."

"Doesn't your dad mind?"

"What can he say? I have the house all cleaned on Friday."

"Then what do you do on Saturday mornings?" It was an organized house, all right, but it sounded more like an institution to me.

"Whatever. I walk to the Y with Pete and then I decide. Sometimes I go to the library or the art center or down to the bus depot and watch people. Then I pick up Pete and we go home."

I couldn't offer to share her Saturdays. I had a job bagging groceries.

Then it was Christmas vacation and Mom and I were off for our winter trip to Colorado and skiing and good old Rob Hunter and all the other friends we saw every year.

For the first time, I didn't want to go. For the first time Mom didn't want to come back.

We had been there for five days before I realized I had hardly seen Mom at all. Rob and I were out on the slopes early every morning and we skiied most of the day, and in the evening we fooled around in the lodge with the other kids. I think it started that first night when Rob's parents threw a big party for us. Everyone we knew was there, including Jake Britton. It was nothing special, the party. We did the same thing every year, except this year Jake's wife was missing. I asked Rob, and he said all he knew was what he heard his mom say: that "she walked out on him last year and none of us can understand."

I couldn't understand either. Jake had been a part of our Christmas in Colorado ever since Mom and I started going there. He taught me to ski, and when I was younger we used to spend whole evenings playing Monopoly. He didn't have any kids of his own, so that's why he probably liked being around Rob and me. He was lots older than Mom, but even if he was white-haired, he could out-ski me any day.

Anyway, this year I'd get back from skiing and find a note from Mom saying she'd gone out for dinner and

65

would be back later. That didn't bother me any. But on our last night there I was walking down the street on my way to meet Rob at the video arcade when I passed Luigi's. That was a really neat and expensive place, so dark you could barely read the menu, full of red and white-checked tablecloths and Chianti bottles with candles stuck in them. Mom and Jake were sitting right next to the window, candlelight shining on their faces.

I stopped and stared. It was like looking at a movie. They didn't notice me at all. They were too busy talking and looking at each other. There were other couples, too, but I figured most of them had been married forever. If you've ever noticed, married people sit and eat and don't talk—as if they were strangers and the hostess had accidentally seated them together. Jake and Mom didn't look like strangers.

When I finally got back to our condo, Mom wasn't there. I watched the ten o'clock news and the late show and the late, late show, and Mom still wasn't home. I knew it took a long time to have dinner at Luigi's, but this was ridiculous.

I started thinking of all the bad things that could happen. I wondered if they'd decided to take a ride up to the ridge. It was snowing, and I knew what those mountain roads were like when a sudden blizzard blew in. The later it got, the more disasters I thought of: everything from avalanches to mass murders. I'd almost talked myself into calling the police when I heard Mom laugh. She was still laughing when she walked in, but she quit laughing when she saw me.

"What on earth are you doing up? It's almost three-thirty. I'll never get you out of bed in time to make the plane."

I had always known Mom was pretty, but that night she looked beautiful.

"It's too bad we have to go back. I'd love to stay another week," she said as she hung up her coat and started for her bedroom.

"Where were you? I thought something happened."

"Why, Chipster, my love, you're sounding like a disapproving parent. Something did happen. I had dinner with Jake and we went out dancing."

"Dancing!" My voice cracked.

"Yes, dancing. They've opened a new disco."

"Jake! In a disco! At his age!"

Mom stopped, one hand on her bedroom door. "When I want your opinion concerning Jake, I'll tell you what it should be," and she did a fast bump and grind through the doorway.

It wasn't fair. I had spent a perfectly lousy evening worrying, and Jake and Mom had been out having fun like a couple of teen-agers on a date. I wasn't jealous, of course, but I was sure glad our vacation was over.

We didn't talk much on the plane home. Mom slept, and I plugged in music on the stereo and made plans.

We got home on Friday, and I didn't have to work on Saturday. I wanted to see Abby and I wanted to surprise her.

Mom said she was going to sleep late the next morning, but I was up early, prowling around the living room and peering out the window watching for Pete and Abby on their way to the Y. They finally walked past, and I waited until I was sure they were at least a block away before I followed them.

It was kind of neat. Of course, I should have been wearing one of those battered raincoats, and I should have had a cigarette dangling from the corner of my mouth, except I didn't have a raincoat and I didn't smoke.

I followed them all the way to the Y. Pete disappeared through the door, and Abby was standing there in the middle of the sidewalk. I knew it was dumb, and I hoped she wouldn't be mad, but I couldn't resist. I sneaked up behind her and covered her eyes with my hands.

She didn't scream or jump or anything. In fact, she kind of leaned back against me and said, "Chip."

I let go. "How did you know?"

She turned around and grinned up at me. "English Leather."

"Did you have a nice Christmas?" I asked.

"Not especially. It was predictable. You know what's wrong with Christmas?" Abby didn't wait for an answer. "It comes at the same time every year."

"It does, doesn't it?" I agreed. "Kinda boring. It should be movable."

"Yes. Christmas in June. Next year in March. And maybe one in August. There should be a holiday that you can celebrate any time you want to."

I thought a minute. Somehow when Abby said anything, it sounded completely reasonable.

"How about Lilian Gish's graduation?" I knew I had to really reach to think up something that could impress Abby.

"No," Abby protested in all seriousness. "That would be locked into spring—like Arbor Day. What we really need is to celebrate somebody's birthday who was important but who has been neglected. See, if the person is important, there's a reason for the celebrating, and if neglected, we have that responsibility . . ."

"Millard Fillmore," I said.

Abby stopped walking and looked at me as if I had just given her the best Christmas present she could imagine.

"You know, Chip, I could learn to love you."

I breathed in so hard my lungs burned.

"But you're wrong. Not Millard. Mrs. Millard."

I exhaled. "How come?"

"Because anybody can find out when Millard Fillmore was born, but we want someone whom nobody knows about. And who knows who Mrs. Fillmore was and when she was born?"

As stupid as it sounds, my second real date with Abby was spent in Collinsville Public Library.

Abby in a library was like a kitten rolling in catnip. At first I couldn't get her away from the card catalog. Then we had to look through all the magazines. I finally got her headed toward the history section, "Listen. We'll never find Mrs. Fillmore if you don't quit pulling out every book in the library."

"I know." She hurried on down the book stacks. "But, Chip, who says we have to look her up? Let's make her up. That'd be more fun."

So we found an empty table up on the second floor over in a corner by the window. Snow started in soft, downy flakes that brushed against the window, shutting out the world like a curtain of white lace.

"We don't even know her name," I complained.

"Yes, we do. It's Mildred. Don't you like the sound of it? Mildred Fillmore."

"And she was born in Secaucus, New Jersey," I added.

"Yes, that's right. Poor Mildred."

"Did she have a problem? A trauma, maybe?"

"Oh, yes." Abby held her head. Abby was at her best when she was acting. "Her parents died when she was but a child, and she grew up on the streets of Secaucus, but still worse . . ." She paused.

"What could be worse?" I leaned forward almost believing her story.

"There was this gigantic fire that ravaged all the records in Secaucus."

"You like that word, don't you?" I interrupted.

"Which one?" she asked, stopping the story.

"Secaucus," I said.

"Yes, it sounds tacky. Anyway, all her birth records were destroyed. End of story."

"Of course," I almost shouted. "And so no one ever knew her birthday."

"Sure," Abby went on. "And Mildred, in spite of her name, was really quite imaginative. She decided at an early age she'd celebrate her birthday whenever she felt like it. She'd get up in the morning feeling lousy and she'd say to herself, 'Mildred. Celebrate your birthday today.' And she would, and the day just stopped being lousy. That's what we can do. Whenever things look like they're going to turn into a nightmare, we'll celebrate Mildred's birthday. You like it?" She turned to me, her eyes bright.

"Love it," I said, but I wanted to say *"you"* instead of *"it."*

And that's how Mildred Fillmore was born.

Chapter Seven

"GUESS WHO dropped in the office today?" Mom flipped enough travel folders down on the kitchen table, one night, to start a general exodus from the whole town of Collinsville.

"A sky diver?" I answered, waiting for her to retch. "Was he wearing a parachute?"

"If that's supposed to be funny, I'm not laughing!"

But she was. I liked making Mom laugh. I suppose it was a way of telling her I loved her without using the words.

"I give up. Who?"

"Abby's mother. She's talking about taking a trip over spring break. South, she thinks. She wanted some suggestions."

"She going by herself?"

Mom looked at me as if I were semi-moronic. "Of course not. They're all going, I think."

"Where you going to send them?"

"It's a bit of a problem. Pete wants to go to Sarasota. Spring baseball training, or something."

"What about Abby?"

"Her mother said she wanted to visit Mrs. Millard Fillmore's birthplace, wherever that is."

"Secaucus, New Jersey," I answered promptly.

Mom looked at me again as if I had suddenly turned into her talented and gifted child. "How'd you know that?"

"Oh, I don't know. Read it some place, I guess."

"Well, anyway," Mom went on, "Abby will have to do without New Jersey because they're going to Georgia."

"Georgia? Why Georgia?"

"Well, not Georgia really. Off the coast. A little island, St. Simon's. There's golf for Dr. Morris and swimming, and by the looks of this place on the map, Mrs. Morris can jog around it without too much effort."

Within the week, Mom had travel arrangements drawn up for Mrs. Morris's approval.

"She suggested I drop them off this evening. I think she wants me to help her convince Abby's father. Want to come along?"

Mom didn't have to ask twice. I felt good just seeing Abby, but more and more I kept wishing I could be with her all the time. Even when I wasn't thinking about her, she was there in my mind like a tune that kept replaying itself.

Mom didn't know that, of course, and I wasn't about

to tell her, although I was pretty sure she would understand. I got home from school first, so I usually brought in the mail, and I noticed that she had been getting letters from Jake in Colorado almost every week. And then there was the phone bill. I wasn't snooping or anything, but we had a rule that I had to pay for my own long distance calls, and the last time I looked the charges to Colorado were pretty enormous—and they weren't mine. The point was that Mom hardly ever mentioned Jake's name, but I was pretty sure she was hearing a tune too.

We went over to the Morrises about eight. Mrs. Morris answered the bell and talked us all the way from the front door to the same uncomfortable love seat, interspersing a quick introduction in Dr. Morris's direction. It was like *déjà vu,* a replay of my first visit: Dr. Morris and his newspaper in the same chair, Pete on the floor, reading a book this time, and Abby off by herself.

"I really hope I'm not intruding," Mom began, "but I wanted to go over . . ."

Before she could finish, Dr. Morris had jumped up from his chair, shook Mom's hand, offered to get her a drink, and hurried off to the kitchen as if he were a professional wine steward.

It was happening again. By themselves Pete and Abby and Mrs. Morris were real, but when I saw them together they were all out of focus—like a blurred photograph. Pete, who was always in action, hardly moved. Abby, who always bubbled with crazy ideas, retreated into that world of her own, and Mrs. Morris didn't just chatter, she babbled as if she were trying to fill up the empty spaces in the room.

And me? I sat on the love seat beside Mom and listened. Mom was good. Really good. I mean she charmed their socks off.

"The place *is* ideal," Dr. Morris said, crossing his legs and sitting back in his chair.

"Sounds charming," Mrs. Morris agreed.

"And certainly reasonable—the family rate and all."

Mrs. Morris smiled.

"There's one problem," he went on. "It's a ten-day package. I can't be gone that long, and it would mean my girls would miss school—at least three days."

Mrs. Morris frowned.

"What would you think, Mother"—he turned to Mrs. Morris—"if you went on ahead, and Abby and Pete and I flew down to meet you?"

I didn't know what Mrs. Morris felt, but I thought it was a great idea. I glanced over at Abby. I don't know quite how to describe what she looked like, except that she was sitting as still as if she were frozen. I don't think anyone else noticed.

"Oh, there's no problem," Mom broke in. "I took that into account. That Friday is Good Friday. No school. The Wednesday and Thursday before that are in-service days for the teachers."

"Oh," Dr. Morris replied, almost embarrassed. "I guess I should keep better track of my girls' school calendar."

In another couple of minutes, Dr. Morris was agreeing with everything Mom proposed, Mrs. Morris was smiling again, and Abby and Pete were looking through the travel folders.

If watching the Morrises was like looking at a photo, watching Mom was like having double vision. I saw the

74

Mom I knew, but I saw someone else too. I saw the business person, poised, knowledgeable, assured. And then as I sat there it was suddenly triple vision: besides the Mom I knew and Mom, the business person, there was another Mom—a beautiful, special, distinct woman who had no connection with me, who existed all by herself, even had a life of her own I knew nothing about. I remembered that last night in Colorado. That was whom Jake must have seen and whom he knew as "Jean," not "Mom." For a minute I almost envied him. Then I blinked and it was just Mom again, putting the finishing touches on the deal.

Mom didn't say much on the way home, but as we sat at the kitchen table she looked up from her brochures and said, "They're a lovely family—but is Abby always that quiet?"

"Not always." I sounded almost defensive. "Maybe she was disappointed when she thought she couldn't go down with her mother."

"You're probably right." Mom shrugged. "But I wasn't comfortable, somehow. Perhaps it was that dreadful love seat. Do you know what I mean?"

"I sure do," I said, rubbing the small of my back. "It doesn't fit."

"No," Mom said slowly. "It doesn't." She yawned. "I've got work to do. See you in the morning."

Easter break came and so did Jake to pick up Mom for a weekend in Chicago.

Mom spent a whole week getting ready. She sent me on nine hundred trips: grocery store, bakery, florist. The only place she didn't send me was the liquor store. I was too young.

Dinner that first night was like Christmas, New Year's,

Thanksgiving, and Mrs. Millard Fillmore's birthday all in one. Candlelight, linen napkins, the works. After dinner, Jake sprawled out on the couch. I noticed Mom didn't make him take off his shoes. I sat in the recliner, and Mom looked at us with a smug sort of smile.

"I'm suffering," I said as pitifully as I could, "from a case of terminal roast beef."

Jake groaned in agreement, his eyes closed.

"If you two think you're going to get out of kitchen duty like this, you're crazy." She shoved Jake's feet off the couch and sat down.

We must have stayed there for two hours or more talking about track, Mom's business, Jake's investments, politics, and sometimes not saying anything. Jake and Mom got in an argument over Lyndon Johnson. He was president when Mom was growing up. I didn't contribute much. Abby and I had never gone any further than Millard Fillmore's presidency.

We flipped a coin on kitchen duty. Jake lost. He washed, I dried.

It was different sharing the kitchen with Jake. Mom had invited other guys over for dinner, but they never ended up doing mop-up chores with me. That's when I knew for sure that Mom's intentions might be serious. I wondered about Jake's. I didn't have to wonder long.

He was scrubbing away at the roasting pan, up to his wrists in scouring powder and soapy water, when he sort of cleared his throat. I don't mean he said "ahem," but something close to it, which is a sure sign that someone is going to make a kind of speech that they've probably rehearsed. Abby had pointed that out to me, and as usual she was right.

I went on wiping the silverware, one piece at a time, as Mom said it had to be done.

"Chip," Jake began.

That's another signal of a planned conversation. If there are only two of you in a room, and the other person says your name, you know it's a preface for something really heavy.

"Chip," Jake said again. "It's been a great evening. You and your mother went to a lot of trouble for me, and I really appreciate it."

I nodded and grinned a stupid grin and waited. He didn't sound a bit like the guy I'd known for almost half my life, but I didn't want to interrupt. I was afraid he'd forget the next line.

"I hope its okay with you about Jean, I mean your mom and me, going to Chicago. I mean, if you wanted to come with us it would be fine, you know. I mean we'll be staying with my sister and there's plenty of room. And we'll . . ."

Then he blushed. He really did, this lawyer and ex-judge. He was almost old enough to be my grandfather, not quite, but with a stretch of the imagination. He started scrubbing the pan again, which he didn't need to do because it had been clean about ten minutes before.

For just a second, I thought about keeping him dangling. Then I knew I'd have to let him off the hook. He was talking to me as if I were Mom's father and he were asking if he could take her out to an all-night prom.

I put down the dishtowel, paused to align the silver in its case, and leaned back against the kitchen counter with my arms folded.

"Jake." I made my voice as deep as possible. "Jean, I mean my mother, is a responsible person. I've given her the best years of my life, and I trust her judgment. You two run along and have a wonderful time. But if you're going to be late, I'd appreciate a telephone call."

For a minute he didn't do anything; then he started to laugh and I did too. I grabbed the pan before he could start scrubbing it again, and by the time Mom walked into the kitchen, Jake and I were swatting at each other with the dishtowel and the dishcloth, making those sharp snaps that make a sting if you hit, and make you laugh more if you miss.

She sent us both to bed, but I think Jake stayed up longer.

If Jake had started talking to me too formally that night, Mom began talking too casually the morning they left for Chicago.

"Guess who I ran into yesterday?"

"Did it hurt the car?" I asked.

"Listen, I could have handled a dented fender."

I knew Mom was ticked about something. She has a temper, but it doesn't often show, except for that little muscle in her jaw that pulses when she's really mad. At the same time I could see she was trying to be calm.

"What happened?"

"How well do you know Abby's father? You never talk much about him."

"There's not much to say. He's all right, I guess. Why?"

"He asked me out for coffee. I figured it was something about their trip."

"And?" I asked.

78

"It was a trip all right. Chip, is there something going on between you and Abby that I don't know?"

"What do you mean?" Mom didn't often set me down and give me the third degree.

"How often do you see her, anyway?"

I wanted to say not as often as I would like, but I knew this was no time for true confessions. "I see her at school. We walk home together. If I'm not working, I see her on Saturday morning."

"You don't meet her in the evening—when you're running or when you go out with your friends? Oh, Chip. I'm sorry. Of course you don't, and there'd be nothing wrong if you did. It's just that . . ."

"Just what?" I felt as if I should hide something—but there was nothing to hide.

"Well, Abby's father got into this long discussion about how young Abby is, what a protected life she's led, and how he is concerned that you're getting too involved with each other."

"Involved!" I shouted. "Involved! Mom, I'm a junior in high school. She's a sophomore. We've had exactly one real date and Dr. Morris took us home from that. How could we be involved?"

"Oh, my love, I don't know. Maybe I shouldn't even have mentioned it to you, but it made me so mad. The insinuations, you know. When I was growing up they'd call it 'messing around.' "

"What did you tell him?"

"Exactly what you told me. That you're kids. That you're friends and that you enjoy each other's company."

"What did he say then?"

"He was sort of apologetic and asked me not to say

79

anything to you, but said that maybe, since you didn't have a father, I should keep my eyes open."

I tried to make a joke. "The FBI'd never take you, Mom, even with your eyes open. You got arrested on one of those peace marches, remember?

She looked at me without smiling. "Oh, yes, I remember." Then all the anger in her face disappeared and she held out her arms. "Come here. Do you want a hug?"

I did. I had to lean over. Somehow, whenever Mom had her arms around me, I still felt like a little boy. "Oh, Chip," she whispered in my ear. "Talking. Trusting. Loving. What more is there?"

Then everyone was gone—Mom and Jake to Chicago, Abby and Pete and Mrs. Morris to Georgia—and I, in the empty nest, felt like a lost egg abandoned by the Easter bunny. It was so bad I found myself vacuuming, dusting, and even doing windows. Abby would have called it a "Freudian Slop," my cleaning.

I looked around the house. I had cleaned everything and it was still Saturday. I tried not to think about Abby's being gone. I tried harder not to think about what Mom had told me about Dr. Morris. It was enough to make me wonder if I ever wanted a father permanently attached to me.

Alone in the empty house, I felt like a little boy who was sent to his room for something he didn't do.

The house was clean, but my mind felt grimy. It didn't take long for me to change clothes and I was out the front door and pounding my way out of town. It was chilly for April but after I ran for a while I was heated up.

In about five miles I was back in town and circling

80

the track for a last sprint. A couple of other guys were working out and a few people were scattered in the bleachers. I was trotting around, cooling down when I heard his voice.

"Chip. You're looking good." Abby's father leaned against the fence and smiled at me.

"Wish I were your age again," he went on. "All that energy." The way he said it, I wasn't sure if it were a compliment or not, but I walked over and leaned against the fence beside him.

"Thought you'd be down in Georgia."

"I'm leaving tomorrow. Didn't take me long to get tired of being alone."

"I know. Mom's gone too. Chicago." Somehow I didn't think it was quite the same.

"You're on the track team, Abby says. Must be a lot of fun. Big star and all that."

Since I had yet to win a single event, I didn't feel like a star, but I was proud I had finally made the varsity squad. I gave him my best Joe-Jock-Shrug-and-Mumble. "Well," I said, imitating the last sports interview I'd seen on TV, "Well—you know—like—I just—like, you know, give it my best." That would have broken Abby up. We did imitations a lot. Sometimes of commercials, sometimes of stuffy news analysts.

Dr. Morris didn't laugh. He just gave me a light punch in the arm and said, "Too bad they don't have cheerleaders for track. That's what I liked best about sports in high school. You know what I mean?"

I didn't know what he meant.

"One thing about athletes, you always have a choice."

"A choice?" I said feeling like Little Sir Echo.

"Yeah. You can probably have any girl in school."

81

That's when lights went on inside my head. Great big, bright red, yard high, neon flashing lights. He wasn't just being Mr. Nice Guy, yukkie-chucking about the good old days. He wanted me to say something that would prove once and for all that I was, as Mom would say, "messing around" with Abby.

I took a deep breath and looked him straight in the eye. "Oh, no sir." I bit the inside of my cheek so hard I could taste the blood. "You see, I've taken a vow of celibacy. I'm thinking of the priesthood."

Dr. Morris straightened and began buttoning his jacket. "You're Catholic?"

"Oh, no," I replied. "Not yet. I'm much too young to be *involved* in anything that serious. Anyway, Coach says girls and sports don't mix."

I waited for God and lightning to strike me.

Dr. Morris looked at his watch—a Rollex. "Been nice talking to you. I'd better get home and pack." He walked away, then turned. "Any message for Abby?"

"Abby?" I repeated drawing on my short-term acting stint at the summer playhouse. "Oh, yeah. Abby." I wanted to add "your daughter," but I thought that was a little too much. "Sure. Remind her that the term paper on Mildred Fillmore is due the day she gets back. That's for history, you know."

"I'll try to remember to tell her," Dr. Morris said as he walked away whistling.

After I got home and showered and was pulling on clean clothes, I felt kind of ashamed. Dr. Morris was nice enough. I'd been putting him on and he didn't know it, and it had been so easy it wasn't even fun. I couldn't very well apologize to him, but maybe I could explain to Abby when she came home.

Chapter Eight

*T*HAT SPRING I got my own car. I bought it on time from Barney's Car Lot. Mom groaned when she saw it, but she agreed to let me buy it.

It was a VW of uncertain age, sort of red with an oversized motor. It could go from a dead stop to fifteen miles an hour in about two minutes, if it felt like it. The speedometer showed 78,000 miles. I figured that was the second or third time around, but it usually ran, and when it didn't, it wasn't hard to push.

I must have sacked ninety thousand bags of groceries to make the first down payment.

I hadn't told Abby about my major purchase. I was planning to surprise her. Now I could ask her for a real date, and we wouldn't have to ride home with her father. I drove it to school the first day after vacation and parked at the back of the lot. We didn't have track practice, and I thought I'd sort of nonchalantly ask Abby if she'd like a ride home.

It turned out she had a newspaper meeting and a student council meeting after that, so I ended up sitting in a deserted parking lot for over an hour before I saw her come out the school door. I kept the motor running. Otherwise, I wasn't sure it would start when I saw her. She was just turning onto the sidewalk, when I rolled up beside her.

I had to keep one foot on the clutch and the other on the brake and accelerator at the same time. The window on my side was rolled down, of course, because I couldn't roll it up.

"Want a ride?" I shouted over the roar of the engine.

She leaned down and peered through the window. Her lips moved but I couldn't hear anything.

I crossed my fingers and took my foot off the gas.

"I said," Abby repeated, "What is it and will it bite?"

"It is," I said, trying to sound dignified, "a magic carpet. A white horse. Actually it's my *new* old car. Come on. Get in."

It took a little time to open the passenger door.

"Slam it hard," I said after Abby had crawled in. "Maybe it will stay shut."

I looked down at her. I had to look down because the passenger seat was minus its padding, so Abby's knees were almost even with her chin. "And watch out when we start up," I said. "That seat isn't bolted to the floor on one side."

"When did you get it?"

"Just last night. You're the first person to ride in it."

"I may be the last." She groaned. It was better after

we got moving. You could hardly tell the shocks needed to be replaced along with the muffler.

"Want to go to the drive-in burger shop?" I yelled. Just for a minute, I had a picture in my head from one of those dumb teen-age movies—the kind where this handsome guy and this beautiful girl sort of whip into the drive-in in this long, low convertible and all of a sudden everyone is singing and dancing all over the parking lot in Technicolor and stereophonic sound.

"Are you crazy?" Abby yelled back. "Junk food can kill, if this car doesn't. Let's drive to Fowler's Hill. I have half an hour before I have to be home. The meeting got out early."

I couldn't believe it! I thought she was going to say she had to go straight home. She usually did. The VW ran like a badly tuned lawnmower as we headed out of town. It took us three tries to get up Fowler's Hill, but we finally made it. I turned the car around and headed it downhill before I turned off the engine.

"Well, what do you think?" I asked.

She turned her head slowly and looked at me, her face perfectly serious. "It's a beautiful car. I'm particularly impressed with the air conditioning. Did you know you can see the ground through the floor on my side?"

"A few things have to be fixed. It's going into the garage tomorrow."

"And the sun roof. How quaint! Does it open farther?"

"Well, no . . ." I admitted. "But then on the other hand it doesn't close farther either. In the winter, maybe, I can tape some plastic over it."

"What is it called?" Abby got out and walked around to the rear of the car.

"George?" I asked.

"How about The Phoenix?"

"Why Phoenix?"

"Not Phoenix. *The* Phoenix. It looks as if it has lived several lifetimes. Many, many lifetimes and has just recently risen from its ashes. Besides, there's only one, you know."

We climbed to the top of the hill and sat on the grass and watched the traffic down below on the Interstate.

Doesn't sound very exciting, does it? Two kids sitting in the grass, watching cars at the end of an April afternoon. Maybe you had to be sixteen to feel the softness and promise of the breeze that curled around us or to know that something special was growing between us just as slowly and beautifully as the violets that had begun to bloom around the base of the trees.

We talked a little bit about the kinds of things hundreds, maybe thousands, of other kids must say: about school and teachers, about the town and what we'd do over the summer that was coming near enough now to be real at the end of a long school year.

That afternoon was special because Abby was there.

There were long pauses in our talking, but they weren't uncomfortable or embarrassing. Abby sat very still, looking out at the world around her, and I sat very still, looking at her.

I thought she didn't know what I was doing, but then she spoke.

"What are you thinking about, Chip? What do you see?"

I knew she wasn't joking because she said it almost as if she were talking to herself.

"An Abby," I answered. "I guess, sometimes, I wonder where you are and who you are."

"So do I sometimes. Have you ever felt as if you were in two places at once, as if you were two people at once?" She pulled a blade of grass and sat staring down at it as if she found some sort of buried treasure.

I thought about her question. "Well, maybe, a little bit. Sometimes when I'm running. I feel my body and I feel my feet against the ground, but at the same time, I'm standing at the finishing line and watching me. It's kind of creepy."

"At least you know which one is real. You do, don't you?" There was something in her voice that I didn't understand, as if her question were more important than the words she put it in.

"This is real," I finally said. "You and me and The Phoenix. Hey, and it's our first flight. Phoenixes live forever, remember?"

"Sure, but they have to die first." She must have been bored with the conversation because, before I could move, she grabbed a handful of grass, stuffed it down the back of my shirt, and was on her feet and running. "I know a secret," she shouted back at me.

It took me a minute or two to scramble to my feet and follow her. I was still feeling the touch of her fingers against my skin.

She was really fast, and it took me a while to catch up. It would have taken longer if she hadn't stumbled over a tree limb hidden in the long grass. Her knee was bleeding from a scratch and her hair was tangled, and I knew I had never seen anyone so beautiful in all my sixteen years.

I just meant to reach down and help her up, but somehow, when I did, she was standing next to me and my arms were around her and I was holding her, and I'm not sure that I was even breathing. I don't know how long we stood like that. At first she was stiff, and then she sort of, well, it sounds hokey, but she melted against me. I guess I melted, too.

Nothing more happened. We didn't kiss each other or anything; we just stood there breathing together, as if there were one of us instead of two.

She mumbled something into the front of my shirt and pulled away.

"What?" I said, as if this were something that happened every day, and not for the first time in our lives.

"The secret! May third is Mrs. Millard Fillmore's birthday. We are going to celebrate, no matter what. You and The Phoenix and me."

"May third is a school day," I said. I knew because that was the day my history term paper was due, a paper that I'd known about since March, but which I had yet to begin.

"I said no matter what." She stopped just as we reached the car. "We are going to be sick that day. Very, very sick. For just one day we are going to be juvenile and delinquent. We are going to be irresponsible. We are going to skip school. We probably are going to be lectured. But, Chip, for just one day, we're going to be kids."

It hadn't occurred to me that we were anything else, but I didn't argue. I pried the passenger door open so Abby could get in.

"Chip, where did you get this marvelous monster?" Abby asked as I climbed in beside her.

"Barney's Car Lot," I answered. "You know, the one with that funny sign: *New, Used, Abused.*" I didn't hear her laugh, and she didn't talk on the way home, but I figured that was because The Phoenix was too noisy.

I didn't know how we were going to celebrate May third, but there wasn't much time to worry about it. Getting the Phoenix fixed took another nine thousand bags of groceries. There wasn't any choice; she was definitely ready for renewal. I was a regular on the track team and when I wasn't bagging groceries, I was training.

I saw Pete more often than I saw Abby. Somehow, because of meetings for her and track for me, we just never got away from school at the same time. Pete was around a lot. She was still in grade school, still playing ball, and the Cubs were still her favorite team, even when their spring training record looked like the longest string of 0's in history.

Then there was Mom. Maybe I should say Mom and Jake, only Jake wasn't around, of course. He was back in Colorado being a retired judge and playing what Mom called "stock market roulette." He might not have been around, but he was definitely on her mind.

She'd been looking pretty grim for a couple of weeks, not yelling at me or anything, just looking, as Abby did so often, as if most of her were somewhere else.

"Hey, Ma," I finally said one night. She hated that word, "Ma," and so did I. She didn't even look up from the magazine I knew she wasn't reading.

"Yes?" She still didn't look at me.

"I meant to tell you. I robbed the bank this morning, I'm sniffing coke, and I'm thinking of burning down the house."

"That's nice, dear." It must have taken two more minutes before she closed the magazine, blinked, and shook her head. "WHAT DID YOU SAY?"

I figured that I'd caught her attention.

Now that I had it, I wasn't sure how to begin. I didn't want to sound nosy, but I knew something was worrying her. "What's bugging you?" It wasn't very tactful, I knew.

"Who? Me?"

I made a big deal of looking around the room. "So who else is here?"

She didn't laugh, and that was precisely why I was asking, because she hadn't been laughing at my smart remarks for some time.

"Something wrong down at the office? Have *I* done something?"

She sighed and leaned back in her chair.

"Maybe I've done something *right* and you're in shock."

"Oh, quiet. It isn't you. And quit trying to be a psychologist."

"It's Jake, then, isn't it? I thought you two had a real thing going there."

"That's the problem, Chip. He wants to marry me."

"Marry you!"

"That's what *I* said when he asked me."

"What did you tell him?"

"I told him I'd think about it. It's all so complicated. I have a business here. We have a life here. You have another year in high school. And Jake . . . Well, Jake belongs in Colorado. That's *his* life. And then there's your father. . . ."

"Mom, that was sixteen years ago."

90

"But you see, Chip, I'll never know for sure. What if he is still alive?"

"Mom, if he is alive, we'd know."

"I know. That's only part of it. You haven't asked me the most important question."

"What's that?"

"Do I love Jake?"

"Oh," I said. "I never thought about that. Do you?"

"Yes." It was a matter-of-fact "yes" that allowed no room for doubt.

"So what's the big problem?"

"Chip, I've lived alone for sixteen years."

"What do you mean alone? What about me?"

She laughed, one of her old laughs. "There's a big difference between living *together* with a son and living *with* a husband—if you get my point."

I got the point. It was crazy. I guess life is crazy. When I was a kid I was always looking around for someone for Mom to marry so I'd have a father, and now that I was grown and didn't need one, it sounded awfully much as if I were going to get one, and I didn't particularly like it.

"I'll tell you one thing, Mom. It'd save a lot of money if you'd marry Jake. We wouldn't have to rent a condo whenever we go skiing."

"Chip, you're about as romantic as a certified public accountant."

Mom was wrong. She didn't know how it felt to be waiting for May third and Mildred Fillmore's birthday.

Chapter Nine

ON MAY THIRD, Abby and I didn't play sick. We played hookey, and we were not sneaky about it either.

I picked her up in the parking lot at school just before the warning bell.

"Why, Millard," she said, opening the car door and climbing in beside me. "You look absolutely carefree today."

I caught on quickly. "Good morning, Mildred. Happy birthday. What's in the package and how would you like to celebrate?"

Abby settled back into the seat. "I have the day's agenda here. You see, we're going on a field trip." She sounded like a Mildred Fillmore. "And when I took the school paper down last night to have it printed I had Mr. Hufford print some approval signs."

"Mildred, my love, what are you talking about?" We drove slowly out of the parking lot and circled the schoolhouse, waving in the general direction of the prinicpal's office.

"Think about it, my dear Mr. Fillmore. Number one, we obviously can't spend the day in Collinsville. It wouldn't be worth skipping school for. Number two, it's our *own* field trip and we don't have to write a report when we get home."

"What's number three?"

"We are going to drive to our capital city and immerse ourselves in its wonders. It will be a marvelous challenge to your driving ability."

I began to wonder, then, whether we were stretching the birthday a little far. Mom would disown me if she knew I was skipping school, but if she thought I was driving into the city for the first time in the VW she'd have me put up for adoption. As for explaining to Abby's parents . . . it was too awful to think about.

"Our field trip," Abby said, as we drove out of town, "will be both cultural and scientific. I have a list of twenty places of interest."

"A veritable smorgasbord of educational activities?" I asked.

"We will sample each one," Abby went on. "At least as many as we can stomach."

I refused to laugh at her lame pun. "And digest the knowledge," I added.

Abby nodded her approval in all seriousness. "Millard, I've always said you're much too astute to belong to the Know-Nothing Party. We must do something to change that label. It has clung to you for years."

"It's a little late, isn't it," I said. "That party folded back in the 1800s."

"Now there's something else we must do as a duty to our country. These stickers I had printed—see." She held up a gummed label. "This says, 'Approved by the Fillmores' and these"—she reached into the manila envelope again—"these say 'Disapproved by the Fillmores.'"

I successfully maneuvered an entry onto the Interstate and moved the VW into overdrive. "You know what I really like about you? You're so much like me that when we're together it's like being alone."

Abby laughed—a laugh of pure joy. She turned and looked out the window for an instant, then, without looking back at me, reached over and brushed her hand against my cheek. It was the first time she had ever touched me—I mean touched me as if she really wanted to.

"They *are* going to kill us, you know."

I knew exactly who *they* were.

"Well, what can they do?"

"Throw you off the track team."

"Or ground us for the rest of our lives?"

"Put us in headlines in the *Collinsville Gazette?* Maybe," Abby added, "maybe we'll be expelled. We could go to . . . You know what, Chip, do you realize that for one whole beautiful day, no one in the world knows where we are?"

We didn't talk much after that. I was too busy maneuvering through traffic, and Abby was watching for street signs.

I knew even then it was a day I would never forget, and I was pretty sure Abby felt the same. Time went too fast, but every minute had a special clarity, as if it were being recorded by an invisible camera.

What we did and the places we went weren't exactly thrilling in themselves. We climbed to the top of the state capitol and looked out over the city. We spent an hour poking through the dusty exhibits of the state historical society. We took a self-guided tour through the art center and used up every one of our approval slips. The only place we stuck a disapproval label was on a tacky sign that said, "If you can't stop, smile as you go by." We stuck the label right in the middle of the smiley face.

Of all the places we explored that day, the one I remember most is the botanical center. I wonder now how we ended up there, but at the time it seemed completely reasonable. I suppose we could have prowled through one of the shopping malls or gone bowling or spent the afternoon in a video arcade. Somehow those choices never occurred to us.

The botanical center is a big, domed-glass building set down by the river. It looked easy enough to get to, but it took The Phoenix four tries to find the right exit off the expressway. We sat in the parking lot for a minute before we recovered enough to go in.

"It looks like a time capsule," Abby said. "Or a space station."

"You're out of your time zone, Mrs. Fillmore," I said. "But shall we enter?"

We were in the middle of summer the minute we entered the gardens. The air was heavy with the scent of tropical flowers, and there was a soft dampness. We could almost hear plants growing. A waterfall splashed quietly against rocks somewhere in the distance, and strange birds screamed from palm trees spreading above us.

"Oh, Chip." She didn't as much say my name as breathe it. "It's a garden of Eden."

I knew what she meant. The place was empty except for two white-haired women sitting on a bench beside a magnolia tree. They smiled at us as we walked past. I think they had overheard Abby's remark.

"Watch out for snakes, then," I said, as we wound down a path almost hidden by huge rubbery looking leaves.

She stopped and scowled back at me. "For now, I don't want to believe in snakes." Her voice sounded far away. I thought she was going to pull one of her disappearing acts again, where the Abby I loved withdrew into some unknown blankness.

"No snakes," I promised. "But look." I grabbed her hand and tugged her to the side of a little bridge that spanned a stream that wound around our path. Together we leaned, elbows touching, against the cool stone and stared down into the water. The stream was full of fish, moving like gold shadows beneath us.

"It's like a ballet," Abby said. "As if they're listening to a music we can't hear."

For just a second I could feel the water against my own skin and imagined moving with Abby through the cool wetness. We watched for a few minutes more, then, without words, we turned away and followed the path.

I think we must have read every little plastic sign, the ones that tell you the name of the shrub or tree or flower in Latin and in English. Sometimes, along the path, we held hands as we walked. Sometimes we didn't.

It didn't seem to matter. I wanted more than anything else for time to stand still, but Abby turned to me and said, "We have to go."

We spoke just once on the drive home. "Mildred," I asked, "was it a good birthday for you?"

She leaned back against the seat and closed her eyes. The breeze from the open windows tugged at her hair. She spoke so softly I almost missed the words. "It's her first birthday and the nicest one she will ever have."

We pulled into Collinsville just as school was getting out. I wheeled into the line of cars leaving the school parking lot, stopped to pick up Pete, and dropped Abby and Pete off as I did on any other day. I drove on home, parked the VW in the drive, and waited for the consequences.

There weren't any consequences. No one ever knew about Mildred Fillmore's birthday. Why no one reported us, we never did figure out. Maybe with all the field trips and assemblies and shortened classes, there was too much confusion or maybe we *had* stepped out of time for a day.

Everyone did know there were only two more weeks of school. The seniors walked the halls as if they were already in college or getting ready for something else; the teachers looked tired, and although they tried to smile, they were as eager as we for classes to end and summer to begin. Our track team was going to a state-wide invitational meet, and Abby had promised to go with me to a graduation party. Actually, it was Karen's graduation. Somehow, with summer school and extra classes, she had managed to skip an entire year. She even had a job with a summer stock company somewhere in southern New Jersey as soon as she graduated.

Those two weeks in May seemed like one of the perfect times. Everything was right. The weather was great— lots of sunshine and blue, bright skies, the kind you dream about in the middle of February blizzards. The world had turned green, Mom and Jake were in some kind of holding pattern that left her looking happy and, as I said, I had a date with Abby.

It was kind of funny really. At school, we didn't hang around together or walk down the halls holding hands or meet each other at the lockers between classes. We talked, of course, whenever we were in the same place at the same time, but we never made a big deal of it. I guess we both thought we had something so special and so private that we didn't want to share it with anybody else. It was as if the knowing was so strong, we didn't have to put anything into words.

I don't mean to make it heavy, because it wasn't, and it would have made a lousy play because there wasn't any drama and there weren't any scenes.

I spent all afternoon before Karen's party cleaning out The Phoenix and washing and waxing it. Everything worked now, except the sun roof, but it didn't look as if it were going to rain. I had just stepped out of the shower and was peering in the mirror to see if I ought to shave, when Mom called up the stairs, "Chip. The phone. For you."

Abby's voice sounded funny, and she didn't waste any words. "I'm awfully sorry, but a . . . I can't go to the party tonight." She didn't sound sorry. She sounded more like one of those answering service tapes delivering a message.

"Are you OK?" I asked. "Are you sick or something?"

"No. I'm fine. My father doesn't want me to go."

I wanted to yell at her or maybe at her father. I wanted to pull the phone out and throw it against the wall. I wanted to tell her how she'd not only ruined the whole evening, but the rest of my life.

"Sure, Abby." I said. "See you around."

Mom walked in as I hung up the phone. She didn't say anything or ask anything. She just put her arms around me and hugged me.

"Abby can't go! She said . . ." I swallowed a salty lump in my throat, "her father doesn't want her to go to the party . . . with me."

"Maybe he thinks that the kids at Karen's party will be too old. After all, she's just a sophomore. Did you suggest doing something else?"

"No. I didn't think of it." Somehow I knew that *where* we were going wasn't the problem. "How come *you* never told me I couldn't go someplace?"

"Abby's a girl, and fathers are sometimes overprotective. Are you going to the party anyway?"

"I don't want to."

"Well, get dressed. You can take me out. I know I'm a poor substitute, but let's go down to the drive-in and have some ice cream."

School was out, so there was no chance of catching Abby in the hall, and I didn't exactly want to go over and ring the Morrises' doorbell.

I was working full time as a grocery sacker and most of my spare time was spent hanging around the phone at home hoping Abby would call, but she didn't. I hadn't talked to her since the night of the party.

I don't know why I didn't call her. Maybe partly because I was hurt, maybe partly because I was stubborn, but mostly because I was scared she wouldn't talk to me. I thought she might have made up that story that her father wouldn't let her go—that she had used her father as an excuse. She hadn't wanted to go at all, and she put off telling me as long as she could.

I had just carried Mrs. Winslow's groceries to her car and was headed back across the parking lot, when Pete ran up. She was taller now and definitely turning out to be a girl, but she was the same old Pete.

"Hey, Chip. You know what? We're going to Chicago in a couple of weeks. I get to see a Cubs game."

"What're you doing? Hitchhiking?"

"Don't be dumb. Mom and I are going in for a weekend."

"What about Abby?" I asked. "She going too?" I hadn't said her name aloud since that night.

"She doesn't like baseball. Besides she's got to stay home and take care of Dad."

"What's she been doing since school's out? I haven't seen her around."

"Dad's office girl is on vacation. Abby's filling in. She's even getting paid."

The store manager was standing in the window frowning at me.

"I got to run, Pete. Say 'hi' to Abby for me," I said as casually as I could.

As I filled sack after sack with frozen pizzas, Rice Krispies, oleo, oranges, and toted them out to the station wagons and compacts, I vowed I would give Abby one more week before I'd call. Then, if I couldn't reach her, I'd go right into her father's office and ask what was wrong.

100

Friday, Mom left for a weekend in Colorado with Jake. The house was empty again but I was getting used to it. By the time I got off work late Saturday afternoon, I thought about calling the guys to see if they wanted to come over for pizza and maybe frisbie golf, but to tell the truth, I was tired.

Carrying groceries may not seem like hard work, but I'd put it right up there with breaking up rocks in a quarry. Anyway, I ate a perfectly rotten TV dinner and fell asleep with the sterco playing.

The phone woke me—it must have been after midnight. At first I thought it was some kind of joke. All I heard was somebody breathing. I was ready to hang up when Abby spoke. She didn't speak exactly, she whispered.

"Meet me in the park tomorrow afternoon. Please. I need to talk to you. Chip, I'm scared."

I didn't have a chance to answer before she hung up.

Chapter Ten

ABBY HAD said "afternoon." I didn't know for sure when her afternoon started, but to be certain not to miss her, I ran down to the park a little before twelve. I wished Mom had been home, but I didn't have anything to tell her, except that if Abby said she was scared, it had to be something pretty bad.

I ended up sitting in the swing and thinking about all the awful things that might be happening. Maybe her father had a heart attack or her mother discovered she had cancer. Maybe Pete or even Abby had leukemia or one of those awful diseases. Maybe they'd lost all their money. But those were all things you read about in newspapers. They never really happened to anyone you knew.

The park was quiet. I guess everyone was home eating

Sunday dinner. It must have been sometime after one o'clock when I heard voices from the ball diamond. I looked up and saw Abby coming toward me. She wasn't hurrying. She just looked like a pretty girl walking in a park on Sunday afternoon. If she hadn't been there, I would have thought I dreamed the phone call.

"Hi," she said, sitting down in the swing next to mine. "Pete's team is ahead, two to nothing and it's only the first inning."

For an instant I was mad. I mean really angry. I hadn't slept last night. I'd spent the entire morning pacing through the house waiting for afternoon and nearly two hours sitting in a dumb kid's swing, and here was Abby acting as if there was nothing unusual about a midnight phone call.

"Rah, Rah for Pete's team," I said.

Abby ignored my sarcasm. "How's your mom?" she asked. She was sounding like the adult twelve-year old I had met that first day in the park.

"You'd have to ask Jake. She's in Colorado for the weekend."

A roar came from the direction of the diamond. "They must have scored another run." Abby gave her swing a push with her foot.

"Hooray for them," I remarked.

We must have sat there for ten minutes with Abby making absolutely un-Abby-like conversation and me answering with grunts and monosyllables.

Finally, I couldn't stand it any longer. "Mildred Fillmore," I said jumping out of the swing and giving it a push that sent it almost over the iron frame. "What's going on? Or am I crazy?"

103

"Crazy?" she repeated and stopped swinging. "Mom and Pete are going to Chicago in a couple of weeks."

"Yea," I said. "I know. Pete told me. So what?"

"So I'll be staying home with my father." She said the words as carefully as if she were translating from another language.

"So what, Mildred? You don't even like baseball."

When she began talking, her voice sounded like a ventriloquist's dummy, as if the words were coming out of her mouth but someone else was saying them. "There are some things about Mildred you don't know. Some things Mildred isn't sure of herself. It started when she was a little girl. A very little girl."

"Back in Secaucus?" I asked. I wasn't laughing.

"Mildred must have been four or five," Abby continued. "She used to have these nightmares. At least she thought they were nightmares. Sometimes, you know, it's hard to decide whether you're asleep or awake when you're little. Anyway, there'd be this man in her room. Sometimes just standing in the doorway or at the foot of her bed. Sometimes bending over her. Sometimes sitting on the bed and touching her."

"That's an awful dream for a kid to have," I said.

"Mildred thought she was awake. That's why she tried so hard to stay asleep when she felt the hands."

"Maybe it was just someone seeing if she were all right."

"Chip! His hands were inside my pajamas between my legs! Then it got worse."

"The nightmares, you mean?" I swear I heard her words but I didn't want to know what she was saying.

"It is a nightmare, all right, but it's real. It's my *father*."

104

My stomach knotted and I could feel something rising in my throat. For a minute I thought I was going to throw up all over myself and the dust beneath the playground swings. It took a long time before I could swallow enough to speak. "You mean . . . your father . . . he's . . . wants to . . ." I couldn't finish "Are you sure?"

"Am I sure?" Her voice was old and tired and bitter. "I wasn't sure when I was little. I am sure now."

"He hasn't actually . . ." I wanted to say "raped you," but I couldn't get the words out.

"He has . . . , she began."

I could hardly hear her.

"Actually." Her voice was dry.

I couldn't look at her. I couldn't have seen her if I had looked. I grabbed the steel post with both my hands, pressed my head against it, and closed my eyes so tightly that there was nothing but shooting sparks behind my eyelids. I doubled up my fists and pounded the post.

"I've tried to stop him! I told him it couldn't happen again. But I'm so frightened for Pete. And Chip . . ." Her voice broke. "I'll be alone with him that weekend."

All I could think of was Abby's father standing by the edge of the high school track saying, "I bet you could *have* any girl you want." If he had walked up to us there in the park, I would have killed him with my hands!

"Do you hate me, Chip?"

"Hate you!" I still couldn't look at her. I was afraid of what I might imagine. "I hate all right! Not *you*! It's that . . . that . . ." Not even the words I'd learned in the locker room fit what I felt.

I finally looked at Abby. "Have you told your mother?"

"I've tried. But she couldn't hear me. It's all mixed-up. We're a family. He's my father, and he's her husband."

"You're telling *me*! Why?"

"Because there isn't anyone else. Who would believe me?"

I walked up beside her and smoothed her hair back from her forehead the way Mom used to touch me when I was a little boy and sick. It wasn't much, but it was the most I could think of to do. "I believe you, Abby. I believe you."

"Hey!" Pete yelled, running toward us. "We beat them six to nothing. I hit two home runs!"

"Look, Abby," I said before Pete reached the swings. "I've got to think. I'll call you tomorrow. Don't be alone with him. Don't go to the office. Can't you be sick? Can't you lock your bedroom door?"

"There aren't any locks."

Pete gave us an inning by inning description of the ball game and finally said, "Come on, Abby. Let's go home."

I watched them walk away. Two sisters out of an all-American magazine advertisement.

I went home, stripped to my shorts, lay down on my bed, buried my head in the pillow, and cried until my eyes were dry.

It was past six before I got up, took a shower, and sat in the living room to wait for Mom. She wasn't due in until eleven. It was the longest, loneliest five hours I ever spent.

I tried to erase Abby's words. It didn't work.

Maybe Abby just imagined it, and it was some crazy mixed-up nightmare after all. I'd had bad dreams of

106

somebody in my room when I was little, but it always turned out to be my bathrobe hanging on the door or a shadow of the tree outside my window. But the touching—the kind of touching she talked about—couldn't be a dream. And she had said there was more.

Abby was beautiful, that was for sure, and there were many times I wanted to hold her . . . but I was *me*, not her father; and what about Pete? All those Saturday mornings when Abby got Pete out of the house for swimming or took her to the park . . . Things like this just didn't happen. Oh, maybe in really poor families or with alcoholics or drug pushers, but not with families who lived just down the street, not to girls like Abby. If it was true, how could Mrs. Morris not know it, and if she knew it, how could she let it happen?

It was insane. The whole thing was insane. It was sick and it was dirty.

Why did Abby let it happen? I thought of her fingers against my cheek, and I felt sick all over again, this time with myself. It wasn't Abby's fault.

I tried to remember everything that had happened since I'd met Abby that long ago day, and little bits and pieces that had never made any sense started to fit together in a pattern. The watch she hated, but wore. The odd adult way she spoke sometimes. The times she disappeared inside herself. The space she almost always kept between us. Most of all how she talked about being two people at the same time and why being Mildred was so important.

It wasn't as if she were an adult and could sue him or something. I remembered the car lot sign I'd told Abby about: *New, Used, Abused.* How funny I had thought it was. I winced. No wonder Abby hadn't laughed. It was the story of her life.

I was beginning to feel like Abby—frightened and not knowing what to do.

I was still sitting there in the dark when Mom walked in, switched on the lights, and came as close to screaming as she ever had.

"You scared me. What are you doing down here in the dark?" Everything I'd been feeling must have shown on my face.

"Did you have an accident? Are you all right? Has something happened to Jake?"

I couldn't talk. The only thing I could do was shake my head. I didn't even have any tears left.

She sat down beside me and took my hands in both of hers. "Oh, my love, tell me. Nothing could be as bad as you look."

"It's Abby," I managed to say.

"Is she hurt? Chip, she's not. . . . Oh, of course, she's not."

"Pregnant? Mom, I haven't even kissed her. It's not me." I swallowed hard. "It's her father."

Then I said the ugliest word in the language. "Incest."

I wondered if what I saw in my mother's face was what Abby saw in mine when she told me. I never thought someone's eyes could really widen in shock. Mom's did, and her face turned almost as white as the frilly blouse she was wearing. She let go of my hands and pressed her fingers against her cheeks as if she were trying to make sure she was real.

"Are you sure? How do you know?"

"Abby told me this afternoon."

"Does her mother know?"

"Her mother doesn't listen, or can't listen, or won't listen. Mom, we've got to do something. She's there in that house with him tonight, and Pete and her Mom are going to Chicago, and they're going to leave Abby and him alone."

"Begin at the beginning."

So I did. I told her about the phone call and everything, word for word, that Abby had told to me. I even told her things that puzzled me about Abby that made sense now. I didn't want to remember, but it was something I'd never forget.

I thought it would be hard saying the words aloud, but it wasn't, probably because I was talking to Mom.

"What can we do?"

"Nothing right now. I've got to have a couple of minutes to think. Let me unpack my suitcase and get into some other clothes. Why don't you make us a pot of coffee?"

It seemed like hours before the coffee was done and Mom was back in the kitchen. She looked older, somehow, and I suppose I did too. When she spoke, her voice wasn't as sure as it usually was, more as if she were trying out ideas as she put them into words.

"The easiest thing to do is the one thing we can't do. Ignore it. Say it's a family problem, say it's none of our business and forget about it."

"I'll never forget," I said.

"Neither will I," Mom agreed. "So that leaves us with what? Abby will have to talk to her mother. Maybe together the two of them could talk to Dr. Morris."

"But she's already tried that, and it doesn't work."

"She has to tell someone. What about one of the counselors at school?"

"The only one who could begin to understand might be Mrs. Bernholdt, but she's gone for the summer."

"Maybe a minister . . ."

"I'm not sure they belong to a church."

With every suggestion Mom made, I felt as if we were pushing Abby closer to the edge of a cliff.

"I'm not much help, am I? It's just that I've never run into anything like this before. It's so hard to understand . . ." Mom had not even tasted her coffee. "And, God, Chip. What must it be like for Abby?"

I tried not to imagine.

"I suppose . . . maybe," I began. "You think . . . we should go to the police?"

Mom nodded slowly. "Yes, but there must be another way." She picked up her cup, then set it down so hard it slopped coffee into the saucer. "Human Services. Child Abuse Center. Sexual Abuse Centers."

"But what happens to Abby if she goes there?"

"I don't know. Look at it this way: what happens if she doesn't? I guess only a lawyer would know. I think there are court hearings and court orders."

"Jake!" I said, slapping the table.

Mom closed her eyes for a minute. "Of course. We'll call him."

"Now?" It was three o'clock in the morning. That would make it two in Colorado.

"Now," she said. "Do you want me to talk to him?"

Sure, I wanted Mom to talk to him and tell him everything I didn't want to say again, and then I wanted Mom and Jake to take care of everything and make the world

110

all right as if nothing had ever happened. After all, they were adults and Abby and I were just kids.

"No!" I said. "You call him. I'll talk to him. I guess I have to grow up sometime."

"I think you already have," Mom said, reaching for the phone.

Chapter Eleven

"*Y*OU'D BETTER get up." Mom rattled my bedroom door. "It's almost eleven."

The sun was spilling through the windows making splotches of yellow on the rug.

"I called the store and told them you wouldn't be in."

"Thanks," I mumbled.

"And I'm not going to the office today."

"How come?" I asked.

That was dumb. We'd both been up all night and stumbled off to bed somewhere around four. I don't suppose Mom wanted to start this day any more than I did.

"Because, I'm tired, you idiot, and I'm staying home

because I own the business. Now get dressed. Do you want to meet Jake at the airport or shall I?"

"You better," I answered as I pulled the pillow over my head. "I don't feel like hugging anyone today."

"It was a long, short night for both of us, but get up anyway." She came in and opened the curtains as far as they would go.

"This is a case of . . ." The words stuck in my throat. I'd almost said child abuse, as if it were a joke or something.

"This is a case of you get up before I pull you out."

I didn't exactly bounce out of bed, but I made it to the shower thinking of Jake's last words on the phone. "Would it help if I were there? There's a way out of anything, Chip, if you know where to look."

When Mom left for the airport, I called Abby, but Abby's mother answered.

For a second I thought she'd just come in from jogging, and then I wondered if Abby had told her.

"I'm a little out of breath. Just hauling groceries in from the car," she said. I asked for Abby and she sounded surprised. "Abby's at her father's office. You can call her there."

"I thought you would stay home today," I said as soon as I heard Abby's official, "Dr. Morris's Office."

"I wanted to, but I couldn't. My father needed me. No one else was available."

I clenched the receiver in my fist until my knuckles were white and spoke as calmly as I could. "Look, Abby. I have to talk to you. I can't talk over the phone. Can you meet me someplace. The park? Any place."

"I have to be here all afternoon."

"What time are you through?"

"Five."

"I'll pick you up."

"What'll I tell Dad?"

"Tell him this time *I'm* taking you home."

I wasn't sure whether or not she'd be there, but I parked The Phoenix next to the curb and waited. She and her father came out of the office at the same time. He waved to me and headed toward his car. I didn't wave back.

He'd already pulled out when Abby settled into the seat beside me. I waited until I couldn't see Dr. Morris's car, then I started The Phoenix. Silence stretched between us like a barbed wire fence, and I guess both of us were afraid to reach across.

After about five blocks, Abby finally asked, "Where are we going?"

"We're going home ... to my house."

"Why?"

"Because you've got to tell someone—someone besides me."

"I can't."

"You told me."

"That's different. I was afraid. Afraid you'd guess, somehow. That you'd find out ... and think I was ..." For the first time Abby could not find the right words. She started again, "I didn't want you to hate me."

"Maybe you'll hate *me*. I told Mom. You have to talk to her. She'll understand."

"Understand!" It was that awful flat voice again. "How could she?"

"Trust me, Abby. Please."

I had already circled our block three times.

114

"Listen, Abby. Jake's here. He's a retired judge. He knows about these things. Listen. Talk to Mom. If you don't want to talk to Jake after that, okay. But talk to Mom and see what she says. Please, Mildred."

I think it was the "Mildred" that did it. Mom met us at the door.

I wasn't sure what would happen. Mom hadn't known I'd bring Abby home. Maybe I wasn't being fair to anyone, but I didn't know how else to handle it.

Mom didn't say a word, just held out her arms. What really amazed me was that Abby didn't hesitate; she walked right into Mom's embrace as if she were a little kid with a skinned knee who needed comforting. They stood there together, holding each other as if they were the only two people in the world. They didn't need me.

Jake was in the back yard, stretched out in a lawn chair, his eyes closed, but he sat up when he heard me close the patio door.

"Abby?" he asked, nodding toward the house.

"Yeah. But I don't know if I've done the right thing. I made her come."

"It is right. She needs help. It's something she can't do by herself. *It's a secret that must never be kept.*" He leaned toward me. "Once the secret is shared, the healing can begin."

"It sounds too easy to be true."

"It's not easy, but she's got to understand it isn't her fault. She has been robbed—robbed of her childhood, of her family, of herself."

"Why can't her mother do something?"

"She probably feels helpless. Afraid. She needs as much help as Abby does. Of the two, Abby is stronger. She's shown that by telling you."

I understood everything he was saying, but there was one thing I could never understand. "Why Abby?"

I walked across to Mom's flower garden. The roses looked sort of pale and scraggly. Mom gave up on them every year, but there were several little buds beginning to show.

"There are a lot of Abbys in this world, Chip. Far too many. Just one is too many! There isn't any simple answer. The 'why' is somewhere in a father's mind. What he did is criminal, and I don't mean just legally."

I turned. His white hair needed combing, and he looked tired from the plane trip. "I'm awfully glad you came, Jake. I needed you. I wish Abby had you for a father."

"I'd be proud to have her as a daughter. You're doing everything you can, Chip. This is probably the ugliest thing you'll ever have to face."

The patio door slid open, and Mom walked across the lawn and put her arms around both of us. "Abby's gone home. I think she'll be all right for now, but Jake . . ." She pulled away and started back into the house. "She'll need help with what comes next."

I found out something really strange that evening. No matter how terrible something is, no matter if your own world is crumbling into little pieces, the rest of life goes on as if nothing at all were happening.

We grilled hamburgers on the patio and ate and even joked around a little bit, teasing Mom about her salad dressing and Jake about almost burning the meat. I stood outside myself and watched us and wondered how we could be like this when the Morrises were something so very different.

"What's going to happen to Abby?" I asked after everything was cleared up and put away.

"She wants to talk to Jake tomorrow." Mom looked tired. "Then she's going to talk to her mother."

"Fine," Jake said. "I'll do what I can."

"But what's going to happen?" I insisted.

We were sitting there on a lovely summer evening as if we were watching a play on TV.

"It has to be reported." Jake was sounding like a lawyer. "Either to the police or to a human service office. Then there'll be an investigation."

"What if no one believes her?" I thought of how many times Abby would have to retell her nightmare.

"She'll be believed." Jake said. "It happens more often than you'd dream."

"Will she have to appear in court?" Mom asked.

"The courts will be involved, but you have to remember everyone will be trying to help Abby. She's the victim."

I heard every one of the words, but it was like listening to someone read the dictionary or the telephone directory: just sounds with no meaning. Jake kept talking about the "victim," and all I could see was Abby pulling back inside herself, her eyes pretending not to see and her voice flat and dull.

"What if all that happens and everyone in town knows and it's spread all over the newspaper." I tried to keep my voice down. "All the kids in school. . . . And none of it's her fault."

Jake came over and sat down beside me. "It's all confidential, Chip. Whatever is to be done will be done quietly."

117

I yawned. I couldn't help it. Then I yawned again. That's when I learned another thing. Sometimes, even if your mind is racing around in circles, and the last thing you think you can do is sleep, your body just sort of takes over. It was only nine-thirty, but I said good night and stumbled to my bedroom without even taking a shower.

The last thing I heard was the low murmur of Mom's and Jake's voices outside my window. The last thing I thought of was Abby in her room without a lock on her door.

Chapter Twelve

I ALMOST LOST Abby that summer.

I went back to sacking groceries the next day, and when I got off work Jake was gone.

"He flew back this afternoon," Mom explained.

"Just like that?"

"Well, not quite. Abby came over. They talked."

"What did he tell her to do?"

"He told her she didn't have to do anything."

"Not do anything!" I was getting mad again.

"That it was our obligation, Jake's and mine. Not a legal obligation but a moral one, to call for professional help."

"You mean the police?" I had a picture of a sheriff's car and an officer in uniform dangling handcuffs from his waist, walking up to Abby's house.

"No. Human services. Abby stopped him from calling."

"What do you mean stopped him? She's just a kid, Mom. She needs people to help her."

"Yes, I know," Mom agreed, "but in spite of everything, Abby is a strong young woman. Probably stronger than I would have been if I were in her place."

"What's she going to do? What's going to happen?"

"Abby said she was going to have to talk to her mother and that the two of them would go for help."

"But we can't make Abby do it all by herself."

"I know, Chip, but we have to let her try."

"Maybe I'll call her." I had to talk to Abby. I had to let her know she wasn't alone.

"Not right now," Mom insisted. "Give her some time. Jake promised Abby we'd wait until she had talked to her mother."

Wait! Abby couldn't wait. She had waited too long already. If someone held up a bank, you wouldn't wait until he came back and did it again.

The call came later that night. I turned down my stereo and stood out in the hall and listened as Mom answered the phone.

"Yes. Oh, yes. I see. Oh, I think that can be arranged. Of course. Yes, I understand."

Nothing was more frustrating than trying to fill in the end of one of Mom's telephone conversations.

"Oh, I agree. Certainly. No problem. No, not at all. Can I call you back tomorrow? Yes. Will do. Yes. And thank you."

"Jake?" I asked.

"Abby's mother." She ran her fingers through her hair. She did that when she was being the business person. "She wants a flight out to Chicago tomorrow. For three."

"For three?"

"Abby's going."

"Abby going to a Cub's game!"

Then I knew what Abby had done. She had made her mother believe her.

I wanted to call Abby even more, now, but Mom stayed up late working and I couldn't even get close to the phone. What I really wanted was for Abby to call me.

She didn't. So I figured I'd wait until I got to work and call her from there, but sometimes what you decide to do the night before isn't what you do the next morning. I'd get as far as the phone in the back room at work, and all I could see was a frightened Abby and Dr. Morris, "Mr. Good Guy," standing behind her, hand on her shoulder saying, "She's mine."

When I did call, there was no answer.

Abby left for Chicago, and she and Pete and Mrs. Morris stayed a week, two weeks, three weeks, and the lovely June days—June was Abby's favorite month—burned into a sultry July. I continued to sack groceries for harried mothers herding their kids past the candy rack and for fathers ignoring their little girls and their, "Please, Daddy?" My summer plans for outings in The Phoenix with Abby were thrust down into the bottom of grocery sacks along with cans of tuna, boxes of Cheerios, and packages of chips and corn curls.

One day I looked up from my counter, and there was Pete standing outside the store waving for me to come out. I carried my customer's groceries to the parking lot, set them in the trunk, and looked around for Pete. I didn't have to look long. She had followed me.

"Abby wants to see you."

121

"She does?" I tried to play it cool. "When did you get home?"

"Last night. Abby has to see you. When do you get off for lunch?"

"In about half an hour."

"She'll meet you in the park. You go." Pete looked at me as if she were going to slug me if I didn't.

"I'll be there," I said. "Do you know what she wants?"

"I don't know. But she said it's important."

I saw her leaning against the steel swings the minute I wheeled The Phoenix into the parking lot. Her back was toward me. She looked older, somehow. She turned around when she heard the car door slam, and I stopped walking. If you've ever been to a dog pound and seen the look on a puppy's face, peeking through the bars of its cage, then you know how Abby looked.

"Nothing's changed." Abby did that: started in the middle of what was going to be a conversation.

"What do you mean,"

"I told Mom. She didn't believe me, at first. Then she took me along to Chicago. She said she'd handle it. For me not to tell anyone. That it would ruin Dad's practice. It'd break up our family. That they'd send Pete and me to a foster home."

She did not sound like the Abby I knew. She was talking in one-sentence paragraphs. I stood there like a dummy, listening, but unable to say anything.

"It's no better than before." She stopped as abruptly as she had begun.

"No better? You mean . . ." My stomach was churning again. I stopped to swallow.

"So what do I do now? I can't decide anymore. I've

122

thought of everything. Making myself sick. Getting fat. Running away . . ."

"Running away! You can't do that. It wouldn't solve anything." I sounded as if I knew what I was saying.

"What's left?" She turned away so quickly I thought she was going to run. "Suicide? I've considered that too."

My pulse beat against my ear drums. "Suicide!" I had trouble even getting the word out.

She turned back to me. "Don't worry. I'm too big a coward." There were no tears. "I can't figure out a way that wouldn't hurt." She sounded like a little girl.

That did it! I grabbed her arm and pulled her toward The Phoenix. "We're going downtown!" I said, vaguely remembering some sort of center on Third Street with "child protection" in its name. "And we're going *now!*"

"But you've got to get back to work. You'll lose your job."

"Forget my job!"

We took off in The Phoenix, if not from a pile of ashes, at least in a puff of dust. Abby huddled by the door as far from me as she could and stared out the window, her forehead resting against the glass. I stopped at the first phone booth and found the address in the Yellow Pages. I found a parking place a few doors down from a brick office building that matched the address.

"I'll go in with you." I said as I turned off the ignition.

"I'll go alone," Abby said in a monotone.

I waited. She made no move to get out of the car.

"Is it possible," she began in a small, shaky voice, "to love someone and hate him at the same time?"

"I don't know. Maybe." I had forgotten I still had my

foot on the brake. "Maybe you could love someone and hate what he *does*."

"Or love someone and hate what she *won't* do?"

"Like who?"

"My mother."

She wiped her eyes with her wrist. I pretended not to see.

"There's no other way, is there?"

"I don't think so."

"It hurts."

"Mildred." I tried to sound like a United States senator on an election tour. "We got a saying back in Secaucus. If you can't chew it, spit it out."

She didn't laugh. She didn't even smile. "You made that up!"

"I did?" She didn't think that was funny either. "Do you want me to go in and tell them?" I wasn't sure I was hearing my own words right.

Abby didn't answer. Then she opened the door and got out. "Don't wait for me. I think this is going to take a long, long time."

The hardest thing I ever did was to shove The Phoenix in gear and drive away. I felt sick—sick that Abby had to do it alone, afraid of what was going to happen—that they'd break up Abby's home—that they'd take Abby away.

"Is Abby back from Chicago yet?" Mom asked that night.

"They just got home today. I saw her over lunch hour."

"Has Mrs. Morris gone for help?"

"No."

Mom looked at me as if I'd said something obscene. "You mean she didn't believe Abby?"

"I don't know. I think she's afraid to do anything."

"Then, Chip . . ." Mom walked over to the window and looked out. ". . . we are going to have to."

"Abby already has. Whatever's going to happen is happening now. And I don't think Abby wants to see me for a while."

Mom didn't push it any further. I guess she knew how I felt.

All I could think about was Abby. I kept telling myself that she would get in touch if she wanted me. Sometimes, late at night, I'd walk by her house, but it was always dark. One noon hour I skipped lunch and walked over to Dr. Morris's office. A notice, pasted on the door, said he was gone to a dental convention.

For two weeks, I dragged myself off to work and home again with no word from Abby. Then Rob came to visit. This was the first time he'd come back to Collinsville. I often wondered if Mom arranged his visit, but I never asked.

I took a week's vacation the day he arrived, and from that time on, the wheels of The Phoenix never stopped turning, and its gas tank ate into my savings account, but Rob and I learned about girls and dating and dancing and kissing and touching—but not much about caring. Their names and faces became one Joni-Kathy-Terry-Cindy-Annette-Brandie-Pat-Johnnie, but her name happened to be Pam that August day at the city pool.

I don't remember who Rob had in tow, but I was up on the high board, showing off my swan dive and looking to see if Pam were watching, and I saw Abby sitting over behind the pool fence, reading.

"Hey, Chip," Rob shouted. "Dare you to try a jack-knife."

Abby looked up. I started to wave, but just as I got my arm halfway up, she looked away, and I was left standing like a statue of Mercury about to take off into the sky.

"What's wrong?" Rob shouted again. "Scared?"

I might as well have been. My knees were weak, and I felt as if I were diving off the high tower for the first time.

"I'm concentrating!" I called down to Rob, a little louder than I had intended.

Poised at the end of the diving board, I waited for Abby to look up again. I tested the board with a few little half-hearted jumps, then I walked back to prepare for the dive. Abby still wasn't looking. I focused my eyes on the tip of the board, made a run, came down with all my weight, flew off, did a complete somersault in mid-air, and cut the water without a ripple. I surfaced, swished the water from my hair, and swam over to the side of the pool. Everyone was clapping.

Abby was still reading.

Pam grabbed my arm and shouted, "The winner!" Pam had a voice that could break glass. Then she grabbed me around the waist, nestling her head against my chest, and hugged me. Over the top of her head I saw Abby get up and walk away. I wanted to run after her but Pam had her arms locked around my waist and was pulling me over to the chaise longues Rob and I, the big spenders, had rented for the day.

Something told me that if I didn't follow Abby, I'd lose her forever.

"Listen, guys. Excuse me for a minute. There's someone I have to see." I disentangled myself from Pam's grasp, grabbed up my towel, and ran down the edge of the pool and out the gate. I caught up with Abby just outside the locker rooms.

"Didn't you see me? I waved."

She backed up against the wall. I might as well have been a stranger accosting her.

"Were you waving at me?"

"Of course I was waving at you." I leaned my hand against the wall behind her head. She edged away. I pulled my hand back. Words turned in my head, but I couldn't think of what to say.

"I wasn't sure it was you." She looked across the pool as if she were searching for someone to rescue her.

"Where've you been? Haven't seen you around."

"I haven't been around."

I knew she didn't want to talk about the things I wanted to ask. She was looking every place except at me.

"Is . . . are . . . things all right?" Why couldn't I talk to Abby? Everything came out in a tangle of question marks. Why couldn't I say, "Abby, I've missed you. Look at me. I'm Chip. Remember? Trust me. I won't touch you. I won't hurt you."

She didn't answer my last question, and I was glad, somehow, because I guess I didn't want to hear. "Look." I moved away from her and leaned up against the corner of the building. "Mildred Fillmore hasn't celebrated her birthday for months. She'll think we've deserted her. Couldn't we—The Phoenix and you and me . . . go . . ."

She looked at me for the first time. "Mildred is in Secaucus."

"Secaucus, New Jersey?" It was another question.

"Yes." She looked out across the pool again. "It was a long trip. She had to go back to learn about childhood."

"Will she be gone long?" I would play the game if it made Abby comfortable.

She almost grinned. "Mildred is a slow learner. I think she's dysgenic."

I didn't know what the word meant, but I pretended I did. "Is it curable?"

"Eventually. Will The Phoenix wait?"

"Abby," I said. "The Phoenix is probably the most patient bird in the history of ornithology!"

I could have easily forgotten all about Pam and Rob and the rest of the gang at the pool, but I knew, as I always knew with Abby, that we had said all that could be said.

I didn't see Abby again that summer. There were rumors that Dr. Morris was getting rid of his practice. Somebody said he had a research grant at some university and that the family would join him later. Others said the Morrises were getting a divorce and that the two girls were being sent to a private school. As with all gossip, parts were true.

Dr. Morris did get a research grant. Mrs. Morris was staying in Collinsville with the girls. Everyone in town thought she was a fine, self-sacrificing mother and wife to break up her home to further her husband's career.

On the first day of school I circled Abby's house at least five times, waiting for her to come out. I pulled up when I saw her.

"Hop in, Mildred."

She stood there looking at me, then walked very slowly over to the curb. "Mildred isn't back yet, Chip. She's still in Secaucus. I don't know how long she'll be gone. If you want to see her again, you'll have to be patient. But don't wait for her." She turned away and walked down the street.

I sat in The Phoenix and watched Abby walk out of my life.

That semester I became Collinsville High's most eligible bachelor. The safe date. The perfect pick-up for a last minute blind date. The convenient fill-in for a double date. But always there was Abby. No other girl looked right sitting beside me in The Phoenix. No other girl appreciated my puns. No other girl felt the same in my arms at the school dances. Of course, I saw Abby almost every day in school, but it was always from a distance, and I tried to be patient.

If I couldn't be with Abby, at least I could talk to Pete. I waited outside the grade school for her one day. She came out the door carrying her books and swinging a tennis racquet.

"What's with the tennis?"

She grinned up at me. I think she was glad to see me. "I'm training for Wimbledon."

She was serious!

"What happened to the Cubs?"

"I gave up on them. Tennis is better. It's faster. And don't call me Pete anymore. I'm Pat."

"Oh! OK. Pat. You going home?"

"No. Over to the courts. I have to practice."

"I'll walk with you. You mind?"

" 'Course not. You can carry my books while I practice my backhand."

"How's Abby?" I tried to sound relaxed.

"She's fine."

129

"I never see her any more."

"She's awfully busy." Pete returned an imaginary serve. "Besides we have meetings and stuff, and we have to go."

"What kind of meetings?"

"Oh, family stuff. Besides Abby's on the yearbook this year and the school paper, and she's going out for debate. I don't see her much either."

"Say, Pete . . . I mean Pat." We had reached the courts and I handed over her books. "Tell Abby I said hi."

"Sure."

I stood by the fence and watched her serve. She was going to be a good tennis player. She could run backwards almost as fast as she could forward.

In October a crazy thing happened. I got a postcard, a picture postcard, from Abby. It was a picture of the botanical gardens where we had celebrated Mildred's birthday. There wasn't any signature, just two sentences:

"Millard Fillmore was married twice. You'll never guess his first wife's name."

Abby knew I would head for the library as soon as I got the card, and I did. I spent two study periods in the school library looking up Millard Fillmore, but they must not have thought a wife was too important then, for I couldn't find a thing about her. So one evening, I walked down to the public library. I was leafing through the card catalogue, jotting down the names of the biggest books I could find on the subject of old Fillmore when I heard someone call, "Chip?"

I looked around. Abby's mother was sitting at the table by the window.

"Hi, Mrs. Morris." I tried not to sound surprised.

"I thought it was you. I wasn't sure. Come sit down."

I picked up my notebook and joined her.

"Don't tell me they're piling on the homework already?"

"Not really, but it looks like you're pretty busy." The table was covered with reference books.

"Oh, you won't believe what I'm doing. I'm going back to school to finish my college degree."

"You are? What are you going to be when you grow up?" I didn't mean it quite the way it sounded.

"I was always good at figures, so I decided I'd go for my CPA. Don't you think I'd make a good accountant?"

"Sure. I . . . I think it's wonderful."

"It is. I drive to the state university every morning for classes and get back in the afternoon."

For the first time I could see some of Abby in her face.

"I saw Pete the other day."

"That's what she said."

I waited for her to mention Abby.

"So I see Pete's into tennis now," I added.

"Pete's into everything physical. If she could toss books up and bat them she'd be a scholar. Are there such things as physical geniuses?"

"I suppose."

There was an awkward pause.

"Are you still a track man?"

"Trying. I don't always win. Mostly I'm an also-ran."

"I haven't been running lately. We're a busy family, you know. Fragmented, really. Everybody's off doing her own thing."

I thought certainly she would say something about

131

Abby next, but she didn't. I finally picked up my notebook. "Well, I'd better get going." Then, as if I were asking about the weather, I said, "How's Abby?"

"Abby?" She arranged the stack of books. "Wonderful. Making straight A's as usual. She takes after her father. Me? I have to work for a grade." Her laugh didn't sound as if she thought it funny.

I decided, as I walked up to the second floor, that Jake had been right when he told me, "It will be confidential." It was so confidential Abby had become a well-kept secret. I settled down with a volume as big as an unabridged dictionary. I was sitting at the same table where Abby and I had sat that snowy day when we made up the Fillmore game. I was about to give up finding out anything about Millard's nuptial arrangements when a sentence practically jumped out at me as if it were printed in caps. *"President Fillmore's First Wife . . ."*

I couldn't believe what I read! Her name was . . . ABIGAIL!

I sat there, and laughed. Laughing isn't something you do by yourself, but I did. I laughed until I thought someone might come back and see what the disturbance was.

Walking home alone I got to thinking. It had been a game for me, but for Abby it had been something serious. It had been her means of escape. When she was Mildred, she was real. When she was Abigail, she lived in a nightmare. Maybe her nightmare was fading.

"Are things any better for Abby? Mom asked one day.

"I think so, but I never see her."

"I imagine the whole family needs time to work things out."

"Could be." I didn't know any more than Mom.

"All we can do is wait and see."

132

I decided I'd take Mom's advice and wait and see. Mom was usually right. I'd pretend Mildred really was in Secaucus, discovering her name was Abigail, and I'd forget about Abby. It got me through that first semester, and soon it was Snow Ball Time. That was *The* big event at Collinsville High—the Snow Ball. It signaled the end of the semester and the beginning of Christmas vacation, and everybody usually turned out for it.

I went alone. Not that I planned to, but by the time I got around to asking someone, everyone had been taken. I arrived a little late, on purpose, really. I wanted to go. You couldn't have kept me away, but I didn't want to appear too interested. Mom said I was suffering from "insufferable senioritis."

I stood in the doorway to the gym for a minute, sizing up the crowd. Then I sauntered over to the punch bowl and leaned up against the wall with my plastic cup of . . . grape Kool-Aid.

I quit leaning when I saw Chub Prentiss dance by. I didn't know he could dance. He had made all-conference fullback that semester, and he was even going to graduate with the rest of us if he could make up some English credits. Chub was immune to literature, especially poetry, but on the dance floor he was no slouch.

I stood at attention and practically spilled my Kool-Aid down the front of my shirt when I saw who he was dancing with.

It was Abby! Abby in a frilly light blue dress, her hair caught back by a matching band that circled her head like a halo. If I had ever felt sick before, I felt as if I were ready for the final stretcher. The Kool-Aid gurgled in the pit of my stomach, and my mouth tasted like soap.

133

At first I wanted to run out on the floor and rescue her. My second impulse was to get rid of my plastic cup and get out of there fast, but then Abby saw me. When Abby really looked at you, you knew you had been looked at.

The music finally stopped. I waited. Chub walked off the floor one way. Abby walked off the other—toward me.

"I came by myself," she said as if I had already asked her the question I was thinking.

"You're not supposed to. The Collinsville High Snow Ball is a dress-up, date affair."

"I know. I was busy. Didn't have time to call you."

"You mean you were going to call *me*?"

"Why not? You're Chip, aren't you?"

My head was whirling.

"Do you want to dance? I didn't wear my boots but ..."

"Dance? Of course not."

"Then what are we doing here? The Phoenix waits without."

"Without what?" It was an old joke between us.

"Without gas or oil . . . or us!"

"Then, Mr. Fillmore," Abby said, her eyes shining. "Let us re-tire."

"Mildred," I replied, on cue, "that would be radial!"

We laughed so hard that we had to stagger out of the gym. We both knew it was Mildred's second birthday!

Chapter Thirteen

THE PHOENIX started without a cough or sputter.

"She sounds ready to fly," Abby said, settling into her seat next to me. "Let's go up Fowler's Hill."

I wasn't sure about The Phoenix, but I was already flying. Abby was back beside me where she belonged, almost as if she'd never been away at all.

"We can try, but I won't guarantee a thing," I said, maneuvering out of the crowded parking lot. Snow had been falling all evening, and the streets were slippery. I'd meant to get a new tire to replace the nearly bald one on the rear wheel, but somehow I'd never gotten around to it.

We didn't talk, driving out of town. I didn't know about Abby, but there were so many things I wanted to say, so many things that I wanted to ask, that I wasn't

135

sure where to begin. Besides, just then, all that was important was the *now*.

Before we got to the road that wound up the hill, I heard Abby sigh.

"Anything wrong?" I asked. I could have strangled myself. The last thing I wanted to do was remind Abby of all the things that had kept us apart for so long.

She laughed though and I knew it was all right. "I missed you, Chip. I really did."

I didn't have time to answer because I was too busy down-shifting and trying to keep the car headed straight on the road. I could hear the wheels slipping in the snow, and the back end and the front end wanted to go in opposite directions. Then the transmission started making little groaning animal sounds, and a mysterious metallic clicking came from the direction of the engine.

Abby started laughing again. "I think The Phoenix is going to lay an egg. Maybe this wasn't such a good idea. Should we try to back down?"

"Never," I shouted over the wheezes and clangs. "Onward and upward." That's when we began to smell smoke. The Phoenix gave one final lurch and shudder and stopped dead. "What do you suppose is wrong now?" I muttered between clenched teeth.

"Her timing's off. I think she's molting. Maybe she needs water. Something smells awfully hot."

"Mildred! VW's don't use water." I got out and scuffed through the snow and lifted the back hood, as if I knew what I was looking for.

"What do you see?" Abby stuck her head out the window.

"The smoking gun. I think we have a dead bird."

I got back in and tried to start her, but nothing happened. I mean nothing, not a whine, not a click, not a whimper. "Well," I said, giving up, "she had a good, long life."

"It's probably better this way." Abby picked up the idea without a pause. "A merciful death really, better for her, but hard on the survivors. What about the arrangements? Will it be"—she paused delicately—"a standard funeral?"

I thought about it for a moment. "No, I think cremation would be what she wanted. Besides, I think she's already begun the rites. Shall we go?"

We started down the hill, walking single file in the tracks of the dead Phoenix.

"Thanks, Chip," Abby said as the road widened into a street and we moved together toward the sidewalk.

"Thank The Phoenix."

"That isn't what I mean. Thanks for being patient and for not asking questions."

"Not asking questions?" I clenched my jaw to keep from yelling because all of a sudden I was angry, angry not just with Abby's father or even the whole awful mess. I was angry with Abby, who'd kept me bouncing up and down for almost a year like some foolish ball on a trained seal's nose. Or maybe I'd been acting more like the seal. "How could I ask questions when you haven't even been close enough to talk to?"

"You're mad, aren't you?" She didn't sound upset; in fact, she sounded kind of pleased. "That's good, you know. That's one of the first things I learned—that there's nothing wrong with being angry. Not with yourself, I mean, but with someone else."

137

Despite the seriousness of what she was saying, there was a kind of lightness in her voice.

"You learned all that in Secaucus?" I meant to sound sarcastic, but it didn't come out that way.

"Mildred was in Secaucus. Abigail was in therapy. So were Pete and Mom. We still are, but not as often now. So are a bunch of other kids and their parents. I'm not the only one, you know."

I didn't know, but Abby was talking matter-of-factly, as if she were discussing a homework assignment. I wondered if she were as calm as her voice sounded.

"And Dr. Morris?" I couldn't say the word "father."

"He's getting help, too. I saw him once."

"Oh." I didn't want to hear any more.

"He cried, Chip. I'd never seen him cry. He asked me to forgive him, but he couldn't say 'incest.' He called it 'bad-parenting.' 'Out of control.' 'Loving too much'."

"You mean he's not sick any more?" I knew it sounded like a case of measles, but I couldn't think of another word.

"He wasn't *sick*, Chip!" Abby was almost shouting. "He was wrong! He did something terribly, terribly wrong!"

"It was worse than that! He was an animal!"

"I can't hate him. I hate everything he did, but I can't hate *him*."

Maybe Abby couldn't hate him, but I sure could.

"Come on. Hurry up. I'll borrow Mom's car and take you home. What time is it?"

Abby pulled back her sleeve and stuck out her arm. "My thirty-five dollar Timex says ten-thirty." It was an ugly watch, a big silver dial with a cheap black strap. "Do you like it? I bought it for myself."

138

"I think it's the most beautiful watch I've ever seen."
I said.

A strange car was parked in our driveway. We ran up the front steps. I yanked open the door, pulled Abby in with me, and there stood Mom and Jake doing what kids at school called "suck face." I knew they kissed each other, but I'd never actually seen it. I wasn't particularly embarrassed, but I figured they'd be.

Wrong! For just a minute they didn't move; then they turned to us as if the whole thing happened all the time and Mom said, "Hi, kids," just as if Abby had been around every day for the last year.

Jake came over and shook my hand and said hi to Abby, while I sputtered around trying to explain about the dance and the car and the walk home. I guess it made some sort of sense, because Mom took Abby off to get her shoes dry, and Jake said, "Come on in the living room, Chip. You can help us finish a bottle of champagne."

"What are you doing here? I'm glad to see you, but I didn't know you were coming."

"That was pretty obvious, wasn't it? Your mother didn't know I was coming either. I was, dear boy, doing what in the olden days was called wooing your mother!"

"Any luck?"

Just then Mom and Abby came in.

"Ask your mother. First the champagne. Abby, I know you're underage, but how about half a glass to celebrate?"

"Celebrate? Chip, how did they know about Mildred's birthday?"

By the time the champagne was poured and we'd kind of explained about Mildred and her birthday, I was so caught up with the relaxed pleasure in Abby's face that I'd forgotten my question to Jake.

Mom hadn't. "Chip, you were right. We've been spending entirely too much money on Colorado condos."

I hadn't been thinking of Colorado condos.

"And on long distance calls," Jake added, smiling at Mom like a kid with a special secret.

"Soooooo," Mom went on, "I've decided to make an honest man out of Jake."

Everybody was looking at me, waiting for me to say something, but my mind was like a flipping TV picture when the little sign comes on saying, "Technical Difficulties." "Who's going to commute?" I finally managed. It was good enough, though, because everybody, including Abby, was laughing, and we all hugged each other, and it *was* a kind of celebration.

"We'd better get going," I finally said. "Can I borrow the car, Mom?"

"Oh, let's walk," Abby suggested. "Get your boots."

The snow had stopped and everything was picture-card white: trees, streets, lawns, houses. "You're getting a father, Chip," Abby said with a tight little laugh. "Funny, isn't it?"

"What's so funny about that?"

"You get one. I lose one."

"That," I said in what I thought was a teachery tone, "is called *dramatic irony*."

"Mr. Kruger. Dangling modifiers and all. Eighth grade."

"Ninth grade, remember? I was a year ahead of you."

"I learned a lot."

"From Kruger?"

"No. Since then. And you helped, Chip."

"I don't know how. There wasn't much I could do."

140

"You did the most important thing. You listened. You let me tell you. I kept it a secret for so long. I thought I had to. I thought that was one of the rules about a family."

I knew the time had come for her to talk. We walked slowly. "When I was little, I didn't really know it was wrong. I hated it, but I didn't know it was wrong. I thought that was the way fathers were. But you know what I've learned that is most important of all?" She held both arms out wide. "This body belongs to me. Not ever, no matter what, to anyone else. It's mine. My own. And I never have to let anyone touch me unless I want them to."

I looked at the world around us: cold and white and almost as beautiful as Abby's face. I knew what had happened to her and to her family was real. I still couldn't understand why.

I guess that must have showed in my face because Abby stopped talking and started walking, but this time she didn't leave me; she waited until I caught up.

When we got to her door, she stopped again. "I'd invite you in, Chip, but it's late, and I'm cold, and you'll have to do something about our lovely Phoenix tomorrow."

She handed me the key, and I unlocked the front door for her and gave the key back. Her hand was warm as summer.

"Is it okay if I call you tomorrow?"

"It's okay," she said. Then, standing on the step above me, she reached out, held my face in both her hands, and kissed me, softly, sweetly.

"It's okay," she said again, and she walked inside and closed the door behind her.

GRADUATION

Abby was coming to the end of her speech. She had part of a paragraph yet, then the conclusion, which she had rewritten five times, sending me every revision. I figured I'd better start listening. After all, it was a two-dollar conclusion with a postage bill at forty-cents a throw. I sat up straighter and recrossed my legs, which had become entangled in the folding chair ahead of me.

"And in conclusion . . ."

I had told Abby to delete that!

"We are not alone. We are not powerless. We control our own lives, but if a time comes when we feel alone, when we feel powerless, when we feel out of control . . ." Abby paused dramatically.

I had suggested she pause there so that she was sure she had everyone's attention.

". . . there is always someone with whom to share, someone who will help, someone with whom to talk. We must not be afraid to search for help."

She had finished. I was ready to clap . . . but Abby was going on!

"I would like to quote from one of our little-known and unheralded presidents: Millard Fillmore."

I uncrossed my legs and sat up even straighter. This was not in the script!

"Millard Fillmore said, and I quote, *'If you can't chew it, spit it out'*."

I felt my neck grow hot. Abby smiled out at the audience, her glance skipping just over my head. I had to keep myself from shouting, "Millard didn't say that! I made it up! I told you I made it up!" but everyone was clapping now.

"Wasn't she wonderful!" Mom said.

"Wonderful," I said and joined in the applause.

While the graduating seniors, all one hundred forty-seven of them began one by one to shuffle up to the stage to pick up their diplomas, I pulled at my damp shirt and tried to think of ice cubes and snow. It didn't work.

I swore I'd never go to another graduation ceremony—not even my own. Jake was lucky. He had an excuse. He had to be in Denver for some important meeting. At least he and Mom had had the good sense to get married in January in Colorado. I wondered briefly if she'd like living there now that she'd finally wound up the business of getting rid of her travel agency in Collinsville.

Funny—Mom was going to give up working for a couple of years to get used to living with Jake full time; Mrs. Morris was starting her own accounting office.

Abby had told me in one of her letters that her father was teaching in a dental school in Georgia and flying back to Collinsville once a month for the weekend. I was glad this wasn't one of the weekends. Even now I couldn't have seen him without wanting to do something stupid like smash his face.

The seniors shuffled on and on. I watched Abby cross the stage again. She definitely was not a shuffler. I thought of the poem I'd had to explicate for one of my final exams: "She walks in beauty, like the night . . ."

I wondered if her nightmare were finally over forever—if it ever could be. That last semester of my senior year, and all that summer before college, I'd seen it fading from her eyes. We spent as much time together as we could, sometimes alone, sometimes with Pete, and it seemed to me now that all those hours were filled with

143

laughter and with love. We didn't talk about the past; mostly, we didn't talk about the future.

The night before I left for college we walked back to the park and sat, side by side, in the swings. We had to walk. The Phoenix really had died that snowy night, and somehow, after her, I didn't want another car.

It was one of those soft evenings that sometimes happen in August. You know the kind—when the day sort of melts and flows into the night and the stars look as if they're suspended just above the treetops.

Stupid, probably, but I could feel tears somewhere behind my eyes, and I wasn't sure if it was because part of my life was over, because I was finally leaving childhood, or because I was leaving Abby.

It was Abby, of course. I was eighteen, I loved her, and I wanted her. Abby the unreachable, Abby the untouchable. Most of the time, just being together and talking and laughing was enough, but sometimes the wanting, the physical wanting, was so strong it left me shaking and helpless. My brain understood, but my body didn't.

We'd held hands, we'd kissed, we'd shared each other's minds. I wanted more, and I was afraid to even begin. I was afraid of what Abby might feel.

"Are you afraid, Chip?" She was pushing herself in the swing, her sandals making little swirls in the dust.

"Afraid of what?" For a minute I thought she'd been reading my mind; she could almost do that sometimes.

"Of going away. Of starting school. Of turning into someone you've never been before." She stopped the swing and turned toward me.

I looked up at the moon, impaled on the top of a

pine tree. "I guess so. A little bit. What you don't know is always frightening."

"What you *do* know can be frightening, too. But we're survivors, Chip." She got out of the swing and walked over to stand behind me, her hands resting gently on my shoulders. The warmth and closeness of her was so beautiful that I held onto the cold chains of the swing with both hands.

Then she bent down so that her lips were just a breath away from my ear. "I love you. I've never said that to anyone before, but I love *you.*"

I started to get up from the swing, but her hands pressed me back. "Don't. Let me finish. I want to hold you. I want to kiss you. I want you to touch me. But not now. Not tonight."

I let go of the chains and reached back and covered her hands with my own. "When?" It sounded like someone else's voice.

"When we're older. When you're not leaving. When neither of us is frightened of anything." She rested her cheek against mine. "You don't have to wait for me, Chip. I promise I'll catch up, though."

Everyone stood for the school song as the graduates filed out of the gym.

> From Collinsville High, we face the world
> Full of faith with flags unfurled

Abby and I always sang, "fangs unfurled," showering each other with spit on every "f," but it was so hot in the gym I didn't have any spit left to unfurl a fang.

145

"Are you taking Abby out tonight?" Mom asked as we oozed toward the fresh air.

I looked across the steaming crowd for a glimpse of Abby, but I couldn't see her.

"Not tonight," I said. "She's with her family. Tomorrow is for me—and Abby, my love."